Something Really Terrible

Lara jumped painfully to her feet and flung herself at the rear of the truck. As it drew away she hauled herself in among the grease and the junk that clanked and bounced around her.

She lay low and still in case the Weasel should see her in his rearview mirrors. The flat bed of the truck rattled and banged against its ancient, withered springs. A heavy lump of iron jolted and bounced, trapping Lara's fingers. She bit back the pain and wrenched them free.

Lara tried to think: there were two of them now. She had been powerless against Sean on his own; what could she do against the Weasel, too?

something really
TERRIBLE

COLIN PEARCE

ILLUSTRATED BY ELSIE LENNOX

Lions
An Imprint of HarperCollins*Publishers*

My thanks to Richard Brain who gave me guidance on animal poisons

To my children: James, Lara, Harry, Emily and Ellen with my gratitude for all they have given me, and with all my love. And in memory of Feather, our Irish setter, who liked to sleep on the kitchen table when he could get away with it.

First published in Lions in 1991

Lions is an imprint of HarperCollins Children's Books,
a Division of HarperCollins Publishers Ltd,
77-85 Fulham Palace Road, Hammersmith, London W6 8JB

Copyright © Colin Pearce 1991

The author asserts the moral right
to be identified as the author of the work.

ISBN: 0 00 674279-3

Printed and bound in Great Britain by
HarperCollins Manufacturing Ltd, Glasgow

One

"Check your pockets one more time," hissed Emily, peering nervously through the hedge. "We need as much as we can get."

Jamie unwound his long body from its crouched position to dig a hand into the side pocket of his jeans. His fingers reappeared clutching a fifty-pence piece.

Lara dragged him down again below the hedge. The wind hissed across its untidy top. Somewhere the other side a sheet of tin banged and groaned as it flapped on rusty nails.

"Why all the secrecy?" asked Harry. "This is a public road. We're not doing anything wrong."

"I'd just sooner he didn't *know* we were here," said Emily, holding out her hand for Jamie's money.

Ellen was the only one standing. At five years old she could stand and still not be seen above the hedge. She pointed through it. "Well I think it's all silly. If he's looking he'll see us anyway, straight through this manky hedge. It's full of holes."

They looked. The old, tired hedge had leaves only at its top. Lower down it was dust-dry and bone-brown, and through the skeleton of twigs the shabby house and junkyard garden were clearly visible.

Once, when the city had been a village, this had been farmland. But the village had long ago become a town, and then a city, whose tentacles snaked further and further into the countryside around.

These five: Lara and her brother Harry, Jamie and his sister Ellen, and Emily, lived at the edge of the city in a row of three big, old Victorian houses that had somehow escaped the developers' clutches.

The five friends had travelled ten miles on the bus to this deserted lane. Here they could see the tentacles of development at work. On the far side of the road, across a bare expanse of earth, a bulldozer grated its way through trees and bushes, shunting the wrecked heaps of shrubbery into a pile, leaving naked earth behind.

Behind the bulldozer warehouses were already going up in what had once been a barley field.

One day this tattered old hedge would also be bulldozed aside, and with it the house and its shattered, cardboarded windows, and the garden – if you could call it that – with its docks and nettles thrusting through the heaps of dead, discarded junk.

6

Lara surveyed it. She had a serious face, not given to easy smiling. She didn't frown much, either, but she frowned now. "They should bring the bulldozer over here. They'd be doing everyone a favour if they buried this lot."

The wind gusted and part of the corrugated iron wall of an ancient, rusted shed flapped and clanked.

"Let's get on with it," said Emily, beckoning impatiently again for Jamie's fifty pence. "I don't like it here."

Jamie drew his hand away. "Hang on, if you take all the money how are we going to get back? We have to keep the bus fare."

"Don't be daft. Once we've bought what we came for you don't think they'll let us on the bus with it?" scoffed Emily.

The others groaned. Nothing happened between the five of them that wasn't argued in detail by Jamie and Emily. When Emily had first moved into the middle one of their three houses she and Jamie had challenged each other constantly. By the time the wildlife park was over, though, Emily had learned that Jamie's cautious questioning masked his concern for them all; and Jamie had learned that Emily's constant chatter was only the exposed tip of her tireless search for new ideas, new goals to score. They admired each other greatly, but it didn't stop them arguing.

Jamie's jaw sagged. "It's ten miles, Emily! You don't expect us to walk all the way?"

"We've got all day." She was counting the money as she spoke.

"We don't even know if he's got it!"

"And if he has," added Lara, "we don't know if he'll sell it."

Emily sat on her haunches and looked to each of the four in turn. "Look, we've all heard the rumours. If he has got one still . . . well, at least we've got to try. The Weasel's not even allowed to keep them anymore. He'll probably be glad to get rid of it."

She held out the heap of change in her hand. "Twelve pound thirty. Twelve eighty with Jamie's fifty pence."

She held the pile under his nose. With a sigh he tossed his coin on to it.

"We'll probably get it for nothing. Or cheap," she said.

"Who's going to ask him?" said Harry.

"Jamie's the oldest," said Emily.

"No way," he countered. "You got us into this. You can handle it."

"But you have to come to the door with me!" A small edge of panic crept into Emily's voice.

Jamie looked to the others for agreement. "Okay, but you do the talking." He turned to his sister, nine years younger than him. "And you keep quiet. Every time you open your mouth it's us who end up in trouble."

She flounced. "Tisn't either."

"Shut up. Anyway, wait till you see this guy. They don't call him the Weasel for nothing.

He's going to need some delicate handling."

"How come you know him?" asked Harry.

"He used to come round our way collecting rags."

Emily stood, nudging Jamie off-balance as she did so. "Go on, put everybody off," she muttered. Then, "Let's do it now, before we lose our nerve."

Slowly the others stood until the dilapidated house appeared in view over the hedge. A gate separated them from the garden; a wooden gate, rotted away at the bottom edge, swinging open on one hinge.

They tramped down the gravel path to the front door. The corrugated iron of the shed flapped open and crashed into place. Through the noise and continuing after it, carried away on the wind, they heard another sound, softer, plaintive: an animal sound: a bleating.

Emily stopped them all, head down as she listened. "Did you hear that?"

They all nodded.

"At least we know he's got it, then. Let's hope he'll sell it," she said.

"He *must*," insisted Lara. "He's not allowed to keep them anymore. He knows that."

They continued to the front door with its cracked and peeling paint.

A bucket stood beside the step, full of slimy, stinking potato peelings. They must have been there for weeks judging by the scum that floated on them. A pair of hard, stiff boots, cracked and split, caked in filth, had been tossed on to a heap of paper feed bags that were fused together with decay.

"There's no bell," whispered Emily, nervously.

"Knock then," said Lara. "We're not doing anything wrong." Emily raised her fist and knuckled the door: rap, rap, rap – rap!

A cloud passed across the sun and Emily shivered in the shadow. They strained to hear a sound from inside the house. Nothing.

Harry couldn't disguise his relief. "Out," he pronounced. "Never mind. Let's try again next week; next year even."

Emily wilted him with a look. "Maybe it wasn't loud enough." She stepped up to the door again and drew back her fist for a heavy blow on the shabby door.

It swept open without warning, every loose joint rattling to stillness. Emily was left exposed on the step, a small, vulnerable island, with the others behind. She stared with a start into the narrow eyes of the Weasel.

He must have had another name, but no one knew it, even though it seemed everyone knew who he was. Parents who had been children in the town had always known him as the Weasel. Maybe he deserved the name; maybe he grew into it out of bitterness. No one seemed to know why he was as he was: short and sinister, smelling of dirt and drink. A silent, flitting figure, pale under the grime, with greasy, grey hair which was still yellow in the stubble on his chin. No one ever saw the Weasel cleanshaven or bearded, only with a constant scissor-trimmed yellow stubble.

He squinted shiftily at Emily. Like a trapped animal's his eyes flicked from her to the others. His thin lips were drawn back over white gums and his tongue ran nervously across his bottom lip. There were only two teeth in his mouth that Emily could see. The front ones at the top; weasel teeth.

He wore a stained, collarless shirt. Across the threshhold of the door Emily could smell his rank breath, sour and sick.

She stepped back, trying to hold her breath as she spoke, to close out the smell of him.

"Sorry to bother you," she stammered. The money in her hand was oily with sweat. "We – we wondered if we could buy your goat."

He said nothing, eyes flicking round the group. He belched across the space between them and Emily flinched as the breath reached her. When he did speak his voice carried a thin whine. "Bloody kids. Push off. Garn!" He moved forward threateningly, and they edged back.

She held out the money. "We can pay," she blurted, forgetting she had intended bargaining. "Twelve pounds eighty. It's all here."

He seemed not to hear. He was looking around, muttering. "Goats. Damn goats. Hate the stupid things. Nothing but trouble. Never made a penny out of them."

He looked up at them. "Waste o' time," he shrilled. "Get out of here." His voice dropped to a distracted mumble. "Cost me thousands. I don't keep goats. Jees, I hate 'em."

"But we heard one." Emily pointed to the rusty tin shed. "Over there."

The Weasel's head snapped up suddenly. His eyes burned into Emily's, making her heart pump hard. "So?" he challenged. "So what? Keep your damned nose out of my business."

"But you're not allowed," she persisted. She fished into the back pocket of her jeans and pulled out a scrap of printed paper. "It says so here." She unfolded it clumsily, one hand still holding the money, and held it up.

He regarded it with a scowl.

"It's from the local newspaper," Emily continued. "About your court case. You've been banned from keeping any livestock for five years because of the way you treated your goats. And they fined you. Five hundred pounds."

She held up four fingers. "Four of them had to be destroyed. There's a picture." She thrust the paper forward so he could see the picture of the emaciated, mange-ridden carcase of the dead animal lying at the end of its chain, where it had starved to death.

They watched his face. Despite its paleness the cheeks flamed into purple, showing a network of fine veins. The colour spread. The tips of his ears tinged with rising blood, and his throat coloured until his whole face was a bony splinter of rage.

He darted forward and snatched the clipping from Emily, ripping it to shreds. The wind swept the pieces away. "Cursed kids!" he spat. "Damn kids pokin' around. Gittorf or I'll 'ave yer tongues out."

He menaced them with a raised hand and the group backed away. Emily held out the money. "You take this and give us the goat. We'll give it a good home. We won't tell anyone where it came from."

She set her jaw, desperation driving her. "You'd be in trouble if the police knew. You're breaking the law. You could end up back in court —"

His hand hit hers in a savage sideswipe. The coins showered through the air, falling into weeds and rusting iron, rolling away on the bare earth.

"Out of my sight," he growled dangerously. "Out of my sight, or you'll go the same way as the goats. You come here with yer 'andful of change and expect to walk out with my goat. I'll get more for the skin than that! I hate 'em. Cost me money, every one of 'em. No one's havin' the last one but me. I'll teach 'em."

The group edged away, their eyes wide. Ellen, safe behind the others, was appalled by the Weasel. She had not been close enough to have experienced the full force of his malice. Her voice shrilled hotly.

"You nasty, dirty old man!" she blazed. "We're going straight to tell the police on you. You've got a poor goat locked up and you shouldn't have. I hope they put you in prison . . ."

She stepped forward as she spoke, anger blinding her to the danger. Lara leaped to grab her, but

13

suddenly Ellen stopped. Her voice trailed away as she stood staring up into the poisonous gaze of the Weasel. His arms were rigid at his sides, his jaw stiffened under the stubble and his eyes took on a sharp and deadly fury which knifed into Ellen's indignation, turning it to jelly.

They watched him in silence for long seconds until he suddenly span round, making them jump, and scuttled back to the door.

He reached in behind it and swung back wielding a long nobbly stick, black with age and polished from handling. Emily's face filled with alarm as the stick ripped through the air in a sweeping blow towards her head.

She ducked with a squeal of fright, and the blow passed over, snapping at her hair.

They ran. They stumbled and blundered into one another in their desperation to escape the slashing stick. Ellen was slowest, and as they ran the Weasel gained on her. He swept the stick round in a wide arc, grunting as he forced his shoulder into the blow, giving it more power.

Lara was herding Ellen along, but the Weasel was too close.

"Jamie!" she yelled.

He looked back to see Lara place herself between Ellen and the stick, turning her body to take the blow on her back. She was too slow. The stick glanced off her shoulder, and again off her cheek. She cried out, her hand to her face, but the vivid streak of seared flesh turned crimson in an instant. Jamie pushed his way back past the others as they ran for the gate. Lara was bent over, moaning with pain as the Weasel aimed another blow.

Jamie shoved Ellen and Lara before him, ducking low as the stick scorched past his shirt. Harry and Emily burst out through the gate. Lara had recovered enough to run, one hand still to the wheal on her cheek. Jamie picked up Ellen and fled.

The Weasel swung again, a low blow aimed at Jamie's knees. It struck his thigh with a sharp crack, forcing a howl of agony from the boy. He stumbled, nearly fell as the muscles were numbed with pain, and hobbled clumsily through the gate, favouring the other leg, still with Ellen under one arm.

They ran far down the road, not looking back, before they drew breath. Lara wept freely, shaking her head, holding her hand to her face. "Oh God, it hurts," she cried.

While Harry stood, hands on his knees, gulping in air, Emily gently pulled Lara's hand away. "It's not cut. But it's badly grazed," she said.

Lara wiped her red-rimmed eyes on the shoulders of her T-shirt, sniffing back the tears. Jamie limped up, pale-faced, with Ellen.   "Did he get you?" asked Emily.

Jamie nodded, breathing hard. He dumped Ellen down. "On the leg. It's agony."

Ellen was still fuming. "No wonder they took his animals away. He must hate everything. And I hate him."

15

Jamie bent down, the pain still pulling his face into a frown. He wagged a finger in Ellen's face. "We might have got away with it if you'd kept your trap shut."

She folded her arms and stamped a foot. Tears filmed her eyes, but she held them back. "Huh. It was true. Everything I said. Just 'cos you're too scared to say it . . ."

Harry straightened up. "Not too scared . . . too smart, dimbo." He held out his open hand. "Look."

On the palm were three pound coins. "I managed to snatch them off the ground when we ran for it. It'll pay the fare most of the way home; maybe all the way."

Jamie managed a grin. "Good one. Smart, like you said."

Harry beamed with pride. Emily stepped forward. "What do you mean, pay the fare? What about the goat?"

Jamie looked heavenward, despairing. "You heard the Weasel. He's not interested. Best thing we can do is tell the police. They'll see to him."

He looked at Emily's eyes. They were flaming, set hard, like her jaw. Gradually it dawned on him what she was thinking. "Oh no, Emily. You're not going back in there? You can't be that dumb!"

"Not by the front door, I'm not."

Jamie turned to Lara. "Tell her," he commanded. "Tell her, Lara. Maybe she'll listen to you. It can't be done. The Weasel's hardly better than an animal himself. We could get really hurt."

16

Lara shook her head. "He's a lot worse than any animal I've ever met. Spiteful; mean."

"See," said Jamie, turning to Emily. "We'll tell the police. That's all we can do."

"Then we might as well go back and shoot the poor creature now," blurted Emily. "We can't leave it. You heard what he said. He's going to skin it. Now he knows we're going to tell the police there won't *be* any sign of a goat when they arrive. Not a live goat, anyway."

"I wish there was something we could do," Jamie pleaded with her. "Really. But we can't go back, Emily. Someone's going to get *killed* by that nut."

He shoved his hands in his pockets. "I told you we should have brought Feather."

Feather was Jamie's dog. A tousled, tongue-lolling, rag-bag of a dog with hair in its eyes and a tail that flogged like a flag in the breeze. Feather was hardly ever moved to violence, unless anyone threatened Jamie.

Lara wet her fingers and dabbed them on her cheek to take the sting out of it. "Even he would have had a hard time against that stick."

Emily pouted. "Well, we didn't bring him. So what? We didn't bring Scab either, but I'm not giving up just because of that."

Scab was a cat, a tom-cat. Not strictly Emily's cat because her mother was allergic to cats and wouldn't have them in the house. Scab was a hard, blunt, scarred, street cat, with a soft spot for Emily. He carried his battle-scars like medals:

17

a deep slash across his nose; half an ear missing, the other shredded to three ragged points; a kink in his tail where it had been broken.

Grown men and bullies had been scarred by Scab. Everyone was terrified of him, even Feather; everyone except Emily, whom he loved, and the others, whom he tolerated.

Jamie set his jaw. "I don't care what you say. It's too dangerous, and I'm not going back. I'm not letting Ellen go back, either; or the others."

Emily turned away, hiding her flushed and angry face. "You can do what you like. I'm going back for the goat."

Two

Emily peered through the sparse, skeletal growth at the bottom of the hedge and watched the Weasel as he snapped shut a padlock on the shed door and stumbled away. The wind rattled through the garden, tugging at his shirt, whipping his greasy hair into disorder.

He swayed clumsily as he made his way back to the house.

Jamie groaned. "Great. A padlock. How are we supposed to deal with that?"

Emily put a finger to her lips. She pointed and whispered, "Watch when the the wind blows. At the back of the shed."

Another gust whirled over their heads and into the garden. A corrugated panel in the shed wall lifted in the breeze and dropped back again with a crash.

"That's how we get in. D'you reckon you could squeeze through there?" She turned to the others, and they nodded.

"Easy," said Ellen, delighted. She was the smallest by a long way. She could get through standing up.

"Forget it," said Jamie. "You're staying here."

"Won't," she stamped. "I'd be frightened. I want to be with you."

"Harry will stay with you; won't you Harry?" said Lara. Relief flooded her brother's face. "I was just going to offer." He added hastily, "Not that I wouldn't be happy to help; if you need me, that is."

Jamie grunted. "If we had any sense we'd all wait here while Emily did it. No; best if you wait with Ellen. Then there'll be someone to tell the authorities where to find the bodies."

"If we're going to do this we'd better go now," said Lara. "There's no knowing when he'll come out again."

Jamie reached into the hedge and snapped off a dead branch, making a hole big enough for them to squeeze through. "Did you see the way he was swaying. I reckon he's been drinking. People get ugly when they're drunk. That's probably why he went for us."

"All the more reason for doing it now," said Emily. "Before he can drink any more."

She crawled through the hedge, slid down a small bank on the far side, and ran, doubled over, to an island of junk and weeds. She lay flat, hidden from the house. Lara paused before following. Jamie winked at Harry, rolled his eyes in despair and said, "Keep your eyes open." He, too, squeezed his long body through the gap, and ran to the others.

Twice more they raced from island to island, before they were close enough to make the final dash to the shed. They paused behind it, breathless. They were well shielded from the house, in a right angle formed by the shed wall and a forest of stinging nettles a metre tall. Emily looked back to the hedge. She could see Harry and Ellen peering through at her. Harry gave a thumbs-up signal. No sign of the Weasel.

Emily turned to Jamie, indicating the corrugated iron. "Can you pull that up so we can get through," she whispered.

He pulled hard, and the sheet of iron fell away completely, clattering to the ground. They remained frozen for long seconds, expecting any moment that the Weasel would spring on them from round the shed's corner. Emily kept her eyes on Harry. He gave her the thumbs-up sign once more.

Jamie gently laid the heavy sheet behind them. Together they peered into the shed's dark interior. There were no windows; only needles of light that drilled through rusted holes in the tin walls and roof. They smelled sickness, sweet and cloying, mixed with the pungent odour of stale dung, the stink of drains and rotting vegetation.

"God, surely there's nothing living in here," whispered Emily, peering into the shadows. They moved forward.

Rank, sodden bedding sucked at their feet as they trod through it. The stench was overwhelming. Lara skidded in a patch of slime that had once been cabbage leaves.

Jamie caught a movement on the floor. The movement multiplied as he watched, until the whole floor was heaving in slow motion. He peered closer and the movement became a seething pool of maggots, boiling out of the rank bedding.

He felt himself gagging, forced down the acrid taste in his throat and nudged Emily. Her eyes followed where he pointed. She clutched at his arm, her hand to her mouth. "Ugh, My God, Lara. Lara, look at this."

Lara didn't hear. She was standing on the far side of the shed beside a bench. Her face had crumpled, out of control.

"How could he! How could anyone!" was all she could manage as tears coursed down her cheeks. She was looking at the goat.

It was grey as the shadows; a carcase of bones around which the skin was stretched drum tight. The goat was tied by a short rope close against the bench, head hanging low. Dung matted its coat as it stood in abandoned desolation. Its long ears drooped, its body was weak and wasted.

It seemed not to notice the presence of the children despite the new light from the missing sheet of corrugated iron. It never moved. Lara dropped to her knees, unconscious of the appalling state of the floor, her face full of a deep pain which overwhelmed the memory of her scarred cheek. She threw her arms round the scrawny neck, unaware of the smell of dung and death.

Jamie and Emily were beside her. They, too, were choked to silence by the deep, doomed misery of the goat.

"It can't even sit down," wept Lara. "The rope's too short. The poor, poor thing." She knelt with her arms circling the animal. Its unresisting head rested on her shoulder and she rocked back and forth, too appalled to speak.

Emily nudged Jamie and pointed to the bench. There were two knives on it, and a cleaver. They were lying on a dirty cloth. A bucket of water was on the floor. "I reckon we were just in time," she said. "He's going to be back soon, and we'd better not be here."

She gently shook Lara's shoulder. "We've got to go, Lara. Now. There's no time."

Jamie picked up a knife and cut the short rope. The goat didn't move. Lara wiped away her tears and climbed to her feet. She guided the goat's head round towards the gap in the shed wall, but the creature seemed unable even to lift its feet.

"I think we'll have to carry it," said Emily. "It's just skin and bone. We should be able to."

"You mean I should be able to," snorted Jamie. "Just as well I came."

She squeezed his arm. "I'm glad you did," she whispered. "But then, I knew you would."

She couldn't see him blushing in the shadows.

★ ★ ★

It seemed to Harry the others had been in the

shed for hours. He could feel his pulse racing. "What's keeping them," he muttered, gnawing distractedly at the quick of his thumb.

Ellen was shuffling from foot to foot. "Why don't we call them. P'raps something's happened to them."

Harry shook his head. "Don't be daft. There's only a goat in there. We'd have heard if there was a prob – Oh no!"

The front door of the house opened. The Weasel stepped on to the porch, a bottle in one hand. Ellen tugged urgently at Harry's sleeve. "Do something; do something. He'll catch them."

Harry brushed her off. "What can I do," he hissed. "It's too late. He'll go to the padlock first. Maybe they'll hear him."

The Weasel moved off the porch, forgetting the step down, and lurched forward, swaying. He stopped and raised the bottle to his lips, tipping it back. They watched as he righted it again, peered in at the neck and shook it.

"It's empty," whispered Harry.

The Weasel threw the bottle into a pile of weed-covered, rusting iron. They heard it burst dully against the metal, the sound muffled by the weeds. He swayed and wheeled round, placing a hand on the wall to steady himself. He carefully mounted the step to the front door, stumbling through into the house.

"I bet he's gone back for another bottle," Harry said to Ellen. "You wait here. I've got to warn them."

"Don't leave me alone," wailed Ellen.

"I'll have to. You'll be all right. Just watch. If he looks as if he's going round to the back of the shed, shout."

Harry shoved his way through the hedge, slid down the short bank and raced to the shed, leaping the garden rubbish in his path. There was no time for caution. He flung himself through the opening in the back of the shed, startling them. Only the goat was indifferent, draped in Jamie's arms as if it was dead. Harry stopped in his tracks as the smell hit him.

"He's coming. Any minute. You've got to run; now!" he gasped.

"I can't run with this!" whispered Jamie in a panic. "I'll never make it."

They stumbled into the open, where the wind blew the putrid smell from their nostrils. In the light the goat looked even more tragic. Its coat was bald in patches. A weeping sore spread over one flank. "Stone me," said Harry, aghast. "Is it still alive?"

"We can talk later," said Emily, "Let's go – no wait!"

She spotted Ellen behind the hedge, her arms flapping urgently, waving them down.

The Weasel was back on the porch, another bottle in his hand. Again he stumbled off the step and made his way towards the shed. This time he didn't stop.

Ellen whimpered quietly as she watched him approach the shed door. The others were crouched in the shadows of the nettles. If he went round the back they'd be trapped.

Jamie put down the goat to rest his arms. They heard the padlock rattle as the Weasel tried to push the key in. He dropped it, stumbled against the shed, and cursed. The door crashed violently, rattling the whole structure. The four of them leaped at the noise but the goat remained listless and immobile. The padlock banged against the door once more.

"He could be struggling with it for ages," whispered Harry. "He's drunk. Let's get as far we can. Once that door's open we've had it."

They nodded, creeping away. The goat stayed still. Lara pulled at it. "Someone push," she hissed. "I can't budge it."

Harry leaned his weight against the goat's rump.

At the front of the shed the Weasel lost patience with the padlock. He swore and lashed out with his foot at the door. The sudden noise racketed through the shed, amplified by the empty interior. It crashed through the torn hole at the rear and the startled goat jumped, bleating as it did so. Lara fell on her back with a yelp of fright. Harry slipped sideways, falling full length on his face into the stinging nettles. His howl of pain frightened the goat forward a few steps at a painful, hobbling trot.

The Weasel heard the goat's bleat as it was carried on the wind. He looked around him, scowling. He was on his guard, alert and listening, when he heard Harry's howl of pain. With a roar of rage he lurched round the side of the shed, still clutching the bottle.

"Run!" screamed Ellen from the hedge, her hands to her temples. "He's coming. Run; run!"

Emily was helping Harry from the nettles. He struggled to his feet, a mottled swelling already disfiguring the side of his face. They both ran. Once the goat was on the move Jamie was able to keep it limping along by shoving at its rump while Lara pulled.

The Weasel rounded the side of the shed and saw them racing away. The thin mouth swore obscenely and he blundered after them.

Lara, Jamie and the goat were well ahead. Emily and Harry leaped every obstacle in their path while the Weasel, clumsy and uncoordinated, stumbled round them, cursing as he went.

Lara shot through the hole in the hedge, disregarding the twigs that scratched at her face. She turned and pulled at the goat's rope while Jamie pushed. The goat popped through, bewildered and frightened. Jamie dove after it, forward rolling to his feet as he hit the ground. He span round and yelled to Harry and Emily. "Come on, faster!"

Emily panted up the bank and clawed her way through. Harry, at her heels, received a kick in the nose in his eagerness. Halfway through something grabbed him. For one heart-stopping moment he thought it was the Weasel.

"I can't move," he shouted in panic. A thick stump of branch had caught in his trouser pocket.

"Here," said Jamie, offering his hand. Harry took it.

From the corner of his eye he saw the Weasel's arm sweep down in a powerful throw. The bottle glinted in the air and sped directly towards the boy.

Jamie pulled hard. There was a snap, a long ripping sound and suddenly Harry poured through the hole. At the same time the bottle hit a rock in the stony bank and shattered to jagged splinters beside Harry. Shards of glass tumbled down the slope.

Harry's trousers were ripped from pocket to ankle. The white skin of his leg showed through the flapping, torn threads. A little blood trickled down his thigh where the branch stump had grazed the flesh.

They turned and fled. Emily grabbed Ellen's hand; Jamie and Lara pushed and pulled at the goat, almost carrying it between them. Harry stumbled behind, trousers flapping.

"We'll never do it. Where can we go? It's miles," he yelled.

They could hear the angry cursing from the other side of the hedge. The Weasel was a small man. He would worm through the gap easily. Then he only had to run them down. They couldn't move fast, not with Ellen and the goat.

The Weasel skirted the last of the rusting iron and made a dash for the hedge, oblivious to the razor-edged fragments of bottle glass. As he leaped through the gap a shard of glass knifed through the sole of his boot, deep into his foot. A roar of agony escaped from his lips. Still he clawed his way after them. Blind rage overtook him. The glass sliced deeper into his foot with every stride but he limped heavily on, hurling obscenities. Fury masked his pain as he covered the ground in long ungainly strides, wincing against the fire in his foot.

As he lurched towards them the distant sound of

an engine threaded its way through his screams.

Far down the lane behind him, round a bend in the road, the city bus droned into view; a blunt-nosed double decker that seemed to fill the road. Harry, saw it first.

"Here comes the bus! It's our only chance. We've got to get to the bus stop," he yelled.

The others turned and saw it, too. It bolstered

their will, lending them another burst of energy. They pressed on to the distant stop.

The heavy diesel engine growled louder as the bus loomed near, drowning the Weasel's rage. It passed him and bore down on the fleeing children.

"We're not going to make it," gasped Harry, the words choking out of him as the bus sailed past.

Jamie left the goat. With one final, desperate sprint he reached the bus stop as the bus drew level and droned to a stop.

The sliding door hummed open and Jamie gasped to a halt beside it. The driver looked down to where the boy stood, head down, gulping in great lungfuls of air.

The others stumbled up, gasping. Harry grabbed Emily. "What about the goat? He's never going to let us on with that."

"No choice," panted Emily. "Got to try."

She looked back. Now they had stopped, the Weasel was closing on them, despite his wounded foot.

Jamie helped Lara and the goat on to the platform. Emily could see the driver's mouth go slack as he watched.

"Dogs upstairs, Jamie, don't forget," she called.

Jamie and Lara bundled the creature to the upper deck. Emily smiled sweetly at the driver. "That's right, isn't it?"

He nodded, perplexed. "Here, that wasn't a dog."

"Course it was," scoffed Emily. "What did you think it was, a goat?"

Harry winced at her gall.

"Well, it looked sort of . . . wrong," said the driver.

"Greyhound. In training. Poor thing walked all the way out from Riverdale. It'll be grateful for the ride home."

"Harry," she said grandly, "pay the man."

Harry dug for the money which – luckily – had been in the untorn pocket. The bus driver eyed his ripped trousers and studied his livid, swollen face. "Blimey, what happened to you? Looks like you been dragged through a hedge."

"You don't say," muttered Harry. Emily was urging him to hurry. She could see the Weasel hobbling level with the back of the bus.

The driver twisted in his seat. "I thought I saw another bloke running for it."

"No," said Emily hastily. "That's our uncle. He just came to wave us off."

Taking a chance she leaned out through the doors and waved to the Weasel. "Bye uncle," she called.

The Weasel's rage passed through purple to a white storm of passion. His shoulders shook and a piercing scream of hate strained out of his throat.

The bus driver revved the engine, drowning the noise. "Stand back, miss," he called. "Doors closing."

They hissed shut on pneumatic hinges, the bus clonked into gear and droned away.

A bleat filtered downstairs to the driver.

"What was that?" he called as Emily climbed to the upper deck.

31

She grinned. "Someone's having you on, I expect."

The five of them sat at the back of the bus, the goat sweating and trembling at their knees. They watched the Weasel fall far behind, his fist still shaking, and his angry mouth spitting froth as the bus rounded a bend in the road, putting him out of sight.

Three

It took a long time to walk home from where the bus dropped them. It wasn't far, but the goat was too weak to put one foot in front of the other.

Jamie carried it, and by the time they reached the gardens – going in by the side gate so their parents wouldn't see – he was red-faced and wheezing. It was late afternoon as they filed along the narrow path which led deep into the undergrowth behind their homes.

Long ago the fences between the three gardens had collapsed into the spreading vegetation and the whole area had become fused into a huge jungle of untamed shrubs and brambles, trees and countless thriving varieties of weeds. It was their own private wilderness and they loved it. They fiercely opposed their parents' occasional, desultory attempts to tame it. There was even a ramshackle garden shed they used as a base.

This was where they took the goat. It stood trembling on the bare board floor.

"It needs bedding," said Lara. "And some food and water."

Harry shook his head gloomily. "I don't like the look of it. Do you reckon it's going to make it?"

Lara's voice filled with worry. She wrung her hands. "Don't say that. It's got to be all right, it's got to."

"So, what do we feed it?" said Emily. "And what are we going to use for bedding?"

"I could go and ask Mum for some blankets and stuff," suggested Harry.

Lara shook her head. "No parents. Not yet. Let's wait 'til he's looking better. He ought to have hay or straw. What about if we tear up some grass? It's pretty long. It will do overnight. We'll have more time tomorrow."

As she spoke Ellen crouched on her haunches beside the goat, examining it closely. "You keep saying he's a he," she said, puzzled. "But I thought they only put those things on lady goats."

She pointed between the goat's mud and dung-caked back legs. Emily bent to look with her. "Biology prize to Ellen. She's more observant than we are. It's a female."

She explained to Ellen. "It's a nanny goat. Males are called billy goats; females are nannies. That big bag thing's an udder, and those two pointy bits on the bottom; they're teats. Baby goats suck on them to get milk."

Ellen pulled a face. She peered at the goat's dull, staring coat, stroked its lowered head and said. "Hello, nanny. We're going to look after you now."

She jumped up. "I'm going to get her something to eat."

As she ran out the door Lara called, "Green stuff; docks, grass, get anything like that. Nettles . . ."

She turned to the others. "I'll go and get some water. Someone keep an eye on Ellen; the other two get some grass for bedding. Okay?"

She returned with a bucket full of cool, bright water to find one corner of the shed heaped with grass, sweet and fresh as clean sheets. The goat was flopped in the middle of it. Lara could hear a wheeze in its throat that she hadn't noticed before. Beside the goat was a cocktail of foliage in which the creature showed no interest. Lara tried to coax it with bramble leaves. "Come on, Nanny," she murmured.

"Well, I guess we've got a name for it already," said Emily.

Jamie scooped a little water from the bucket into the palm of his hand and held it under Nanny's nose. There was no response. "Unless we get help I don't think she's going to need a name for very long."

He looked up and saw the pain in Lara's eyes. He raised a hand against her hurt look. "I'm serious. You read what the newspaper said. Four others were destroyed because they couldn't be saved. I reckon we should call a vet."

"But we shouldn't have her, Jamie. We stole her, don't forget," said Lara.

"No way," cried Emily. "He shouldn't have kept her in the first place. He's been banned. For five years. And anyway, that's irrelevant. If she died because we hadn't got any help, I'd feel terrible; wouldn't you?"

A movement caught their attention. Nanny was staggering on stick legs to the bucket. They could see the deep, empty groove between each rib, and the skin-pricking sharpness of her hip bones. She tested the water with her tongue and sucked a little in.

"Let's give her til morning," said Jamie. "Maybe she'll try some food, too. I'll call the vet anyway; get him to come first thing."

The goat stumbled back to its bed of grass and flopped down. They stroked her and whispered encouragement. Time passed and, one by one, reluctantly, they left. Lara was last. She tied the door shut with a length of twine and peered in through the dusty window before trailing after the others, back to the houses.

Much later, in the deep darkness beyond midnight, she crept back to the shed, torch in hand, and sat stroking the drooped head until the torch batteries grew tired and the beam faded. She bent over and whispered gentle words in the goat's long, soft ear before quietly letting herself out and padding back to bed.

The vet arrived shortly after nine. While the others fussed and worried around the goat, which still had eaten nothing, Jamie waited for him in the street at the front of the house. They wanted to steer him to the side gate without letting their parents know what was going on.

The vet drove up in a green Volvo station wagon. The huge rear compartment was full of cartons and cases, white coats, wellington boots, tubes, and trays full of bottles. He seemed young to Jamie, and sunny. Jamie had imagined a tweed jacket, smelling like a musty cupboard, but this vet – he introduced himself as Jeff Anderson – wore a multi-coloured fluorescent windcheater over a black shirt.

Jeff Anderson climbed from the car carrying a small brown case. Jamie led him through the garden wilderness, explaining their concern about Nanny's health, omitting details of her escape from the Weasel. By the time they reached the shed they were chatting comfortably together.

Inside the shed the others heard him coming. Emily threw open the door. Ellen peered out, too.

"Two, three," counted Jeff Anderson. "How many more?" He grinned, tousling Ellen's hair.

"Five altogether, not counting Nanny," replied Ellen. "And there's Feather and Scab, too, but they're not here in case they frighten her."

"I'm Jeff," he said.

"And I'm Ellen. This is Emily." Ellen moved back as the vet ducked through the doorway. She pointed out Lara and Harry, kneeling beside the goat. Jeff smiled, nodding.

Then his eyes fell on the goat.

The smile drained from his face and became a mask of stunned horror. "Sweet Jesus," he breathed. "What have you done!"

His eyes scanned the gaunt sack of the goat's body, expertly assessing the scurfed coat, the caked dung, the listless stance and the dull, disinterested eyes.

He shoved past Ellen, pushed Lara and Harry away from the abject Nanny. They could feel the anger rising out of him as he crouched beside the goat, peering into her eyes, his hands smoothly examining the coat, turning back the lips, exposing teeth and gums. His jaw was set and a hard light glinted in his eyes.

They remained silent while he completed his examination. He stood and turned back to his case, ignoring them. The air was thick with silent fury.

Lara caught Jamie's eye. She frowned, raising an eyebrow to him quizzically.

He shrugged, turning to the vet. "Er . . . will she be all right, do you think?"

There was no answer. The vet snatched equipment roughly from his case, venting his mood on it. He assembled a hypodermic needle, began filling it from a phial held up against the light.

Jamie tried again. "We'd have called you last night, but it was a bit late."

The vet turned on him, teeth gritted. "Last night. Last night! You stupid boy; last month would have been more like it. How dare you keep a creature in this condition. I've a good mind to inform the police. As it is I shall be talking to your parents."

He pointed to the other side of the shed, away from Nanny. "Stand there, until I'm finished." he ordered. "I've got a few things to say to you yet."

They gathered obediently, away from his anger.

"What did you tell him?" Emily murmured to Jamie, wide-eyed.

"Just that we were worried about the goat. I think he thinks we did this to her."

Lara gasped. "Didn't you tell him what happened?"

"How could I?" he hissed. "We stole her, didn't we!"

Ellen was watching the vet. "What are going to do?" she asked cautiously.

He was feeling along her neck, seeking enough flesh on the wasted frame in which to plunge the needle. "I'm putting her to sleep."

He paused, examining the words in his own mind as he said it. He changed his mind and said harshly, "Destroying her. Before you do. At least it'll be painless this way."

He turned towards them, spitting out the words, waving the hypodermic in the air to emphasize them, "I've only ever come across one case worse than this. A man who ended up in court. He was banned from keeping any kind of animal. My God, what do they teach you kids nowadays?"

The short stampede across the bare boards on the shed surprised him enough to stop him plunging the needle into Nanny's flank. Jamie grabbed his arm. Lara flung herself across Nanny, careful not to crush the frail creature. Emily, Harry and Ellen forced themselves between the vet and the goat.

"What the hell —" he stormed.

"You – you don't understand," stammered Jamie, releasing the vet's arm as if it were a hot rock, appalled at his own boldness. "We didn't do this. It's not our fault."

"I thought you said it was your goat."

"He was frightened we might get into trouble," said Lara.

"We only got it last night." added Harry.

"We . . . rescued it," explained Emily.

Ellen clapped her hands with glee. "We stole it, she means. From the Weasel. Serves him right."

They glowered at Ellen, saying nothing, their faces turning scarlet.

The vet surveyed each one in turn, bemused. His features relaxed a little. "Start from the beginning," he ordered.

When they had finished he stood, shaking his head, and put his hand on Jamie's shoulder. "Look, I'm sorry. When you said it was your goat I thought you'd had it some time."

He looked at the others, too, and said, "I know him – the Weasel."

"Was he the man you were talking about, who went to court?" asked Emily.

Jeff Anderson nodded. "I take my hat off to you. He's dangerous, malicious. But really, you can't

40

take the law into your own hands. You should have told someone. The police . . . "

"We didn't have time," blurted Lara, "He was going to kill her —"

Jeff was shaking his head. "It doesn't make any difference," he said gently. "At least you saved her from a terrifying, agonizing death; but I shall have to destroy . . . put her to sleep. At least it won't frighten her. It'll be just like that – going to sleep."

They were stunned, incredulous.

"Pardon?" said Lara, blankly.

"She'll never make it; she's almost dead now. Best put her out of her misery," he explained. "It's not just her condition, she's also —"

Ellen stamped her feet. "I thought you were supposed to save animals!"

"Of course I am; but look at her. I don't think she can be saved."

"But let's try at least," pleaded Emily. "We can't just switch her off, like a light."

"It'll be best in the long run . . . "

"Who for?" cried Harry indignantly. "Try asking her." They all followed his finger. Nanny stood forlornly, head down. "The long run isn't going to be very long for her, is it?"

They stared at the vet in disgusted disbelief. He was obliged to destroy lots of animals. He hated the task; never got used to it. But sometimes it had to be done. Like now. Even so he found his resolve wilting under their disdainful glare. He felt . . . guilty.

"All right," he declared. "All right, I'll see what I can do. She'll have to stay in the surgery. We've got some special pens there. I may not be able to save her, mind. I'll try though."

The children looked at one another. They didn't seem impressed.

"Well?" he asked.

"That's daft," said Emily.

But —"

"She means Nanny should stay with us," explained Lara. "We all do, don't we?" She looked to the others and they nodded.

"She's just spent goodness knows how long locked up. She wants looking after; a bit of loving. I'm sure you mean well, but she's not going to get it in a surgery pen, is she?"

"We can give her much more attention than you, and we can always call you if she gets worse." Lara looked earnestly into the vet's eyes. "Please . . .?"

He spread his arms in a gesture of hopelessness. "But you don't know anything about goats. They're hard to handle; they eat everything . . . anything."

Jamie gestured with his thumb. "Have you seen out there. It's a jungle. Keep her busy for years."

"They break fences for fun. You can't keep them in, even when they're —"

"We'll watch her, and if we can't watch her we'll tether her," cut in Emily.

"She's going to need a special diet, to get her back in shape, and because she's —"

"You tell us what to get, and we'll make sure she gets it," said Harry.

42

"It'll cost money," the vet continued through the interruptions. "Lots of money. Especially in her condition; she's —"

"We'll get some," said Ellen. "We're good at that."

"— she's PREGNANT," he finally managed to say.

Nanny's breathing was the only sound in the silence.

Jeff couldn't help smiling at their bemused faces, lost for words at last.

"Er . . . pardon?" said Emily.

"She's pregnant. She's going to have a kid, a baby goat. In about a month to six weeks, I think. It's hard to tell in her condition."

"Why didn't you tell us before?" asked Lara, wide eyes shining.

"I've been trying for five minutes! You lot kept interrupting."

Lara hugged herself, grinning. A bright light burned in her eyes. "A kid," she breathed.

Jeff watched her with alarm. "Look, don't get excited. The reason I told you was so you'd see it's impossible. After what she's been through she's going to have her work cut out pulling herself through. The chances of the kid surviving are practically nil."

Emily was aghast. "But that's *why* we have to try. Don't you see? That must be why Nanny's hung on all this time. For the sake of the kid. We can't decide whether it's worth it or not. She's already done that or she would have given up, like the others."

43

Lara joined in. "Let us try, please. I swear we'll take care of her, twenty-four-hours-a-day if we have to."

The vet shook his head and knelt beside his case, putting down the hypodermic and picking up another, filling it as he did the first.

"What are you doing?" asked Jamie, nervously.

"She'll need a heavy dose of vitamins to give her a chance. Her and the kid. This is the quickest way of getting them into her. I must be crazy, but I guess if anyone can pull her through, it'll be you lot."

The howl of delight ricocheted out of the shed and through the clearing.

Jeff cleared them aside and administered the vitamins, issuing instructions as he did so. "You'll need hay for bedding. And you must keep it dry. Change it daily. Don't let her outdoors yet; let's wait until we see some improvement."

"Cut tree branches: beech, ash, they're full of nutrition; stinging nettles are good, too. But you'll have to hang them somehow. She won't eat anything off the floor. Bang a nail in the roof and hang bundles from a string. She's an Anglo-Nubian. You can tell from the Roman nose and the floppy ears. They're the prettiest breed, but they're probably the most delicate, too."

He replaced the hypodermic in the case and picked up a pad and pencil. "This is the address of a feed merchant. It's not too far away. Get a sack of this. I'll write down the name so you don't forget it. It's high nutrient feed for ruminants, like cows and goats. Can you get hold of a cart or something? These sacks weigh about twenty-five kilos. It'll be heavy going if you have to carry it."

They listened to every word as he rattled off orders. "Don't let her get wet. Keep her in for a while. I'll be back daily to check on her."

"If she improves . . . *if*," he looked hard at each of them, stressing the word, "then you can tether her in the garden. She'll have the time of her life."

He picked up his pad again, remembering something else. "Get this book from the library. It'll tell you all about goats: feeding, cleaning, milking —"

"Milking!" they chorused.

"Of course."

"But will we have to?" said Emily. "I mean, I thought the kid . . . "

He said gently. "I admire your determination, all of you. If it hadn't been for that I wouldn't have let you talk me into this. But you have to understand: the kid may not make it. It could be – probably will be – born dead. She could abort it tomorrow, because of her condition."

He studied the sadness in their faces and added gently, "I'm sorry, but I want you to understand what you're taking on. So, if the kid dies, you'll have to milk her because she'll be in pain if you don't. Even if it lives you'll have to milk off some. The kid couldn't drink it all."

"How much will there be?" asked Lara.

"Hard to say, probably be low, because of what she's gone through. Maybe a couple of litres a day."

"What'll we do with it?"

"Drink it, of course. Or sell it to your parents. Goats' milk is all the rage now. It's supposed to be good for you."

"We – er – we haven't told them yet."

He snapped his case shut. "Well, you must. Don't worry, I'll have a word with them if they've got any doubts. They should be proud of you. I am."

There was silence in the shed. One by one they moved over to Nanny and fondled her head, stroked her back. Emily opened her mouth to speak, and thought better of it. Jamie grinned. "I know what you're thinking," he said.

Emily blushed. "We could start a farmyard. City kids love farmyards. It'd be a real hit. They'd pay to learn to milk . . . "

Her mounting enthusiasm was drowned by the roar of laughter from the rest of them.

Four

The bus creaked slowly to a halt and the pneumatic doors hissed open. The Weasel hobbled forward and leaned in. He was wearing only one boot. The other foot was heavily bandaged.

From his seat the driver could smell the Weasel's sour breath. He looked pale and sick, his eyes were hooded and bloodshot and his voice bubbled thinly in his throat. He had been drinking heavily since the previous day, reliving again and again his confrontation with the thieving gang of kids.

He had convinced himself he was blameless; that they should be – would be – made to pay: for the goat, for the damaged shed, for his foot . . .

"Were you on this bus yesterday?" he whined through the open door.

"No mate. Day off yesterday."

"When will the other driver be back?"

"He's not due on this run again for a couple of days, maybe three. I dunno."

The Weasel turned aside without acknowledging the driver's words. He limped away, cursing violently under his breath. The driver shrugged and knocked the bus into gear; the doors hissed shut and the vehicle growled away.

They used a set of old pram wheels to pick up the feed bag. Feather went with them, weaving random figures of eight between their legs, tongue lolling, tail flogging the air. Scab, who held a barely tolerant contempt for Feather, sat and watched them go in dignified disdain.

They handed the vet's handwritten note to the feed merchant, a big man in a brown warehouseman's coat that barely buttoned across his broad chest.

The children were silent. They had borrowed on next week's pocket money, scraped pennies from the bottoms of drawers, bought credit from their parents on the promise of work yet to be done, to raise enough money. They hadn't asked the vet how much that might be. They had no idea whether they had enough.

The man strode to the back of the warehouse, searching the stacks of filled feed bags – some of them as high as a house gutter – for the right pile. "Goat eh? Haven't seen one o' them around here for a few years, not since the new estates went up."

He plucked a sack from the top of a pile, tossed it over a shoulder and strode back. He lowered it on to the pram wheels and they sagged and creaked ominously.

"How much –" began Emily tentatively.

He waved them away. "Nothing to pay. All taken care of, by Mr Anderson."

"The vet?" gasped Lara. The man nodded.

They recovered control of their dropped jaws and happy grins spread over their faces.

"What a nice guy," said Jamie as they pushed the wheels away with their load. "He didn't have to do that."

"She's got to get better," said Lara, a note of desperation in her voice. "So we can show him it was worth trying. Feather, get your nose out of the sack. It's not for you."

The dog was infected with their excitement. He pranced and pestered round the pram wheels while they steered it home with its load. It wasn't until they turned into their own street that he grew quiet.

They didn't notice at first. It was Ellen who said, "What's wrong with Feather?"

He was ahead of them, his body tensed, nose forward, back low, his eyes fixed on a figure in the distance. It was a boy, slouched against Jamie's front gate. They couldn't make out the features from the distance, but they all knew who it was. There was something . . . surly, about the way in which he stood, hands in pockets. The thickset frame and the round, moonface in its bullet head were – unfortunately – too familiar.

"Sean," breathed Jamie. He added sarcastically, "Great!"

He called Feather to heel. The dog knew Sean well from past encounters and had good reason to be wary of him. A low growl rose from his throat.

"We've got to go right past him," said Emily. "Do you think he'll make trouble?"

Jamie shook his head. "Not with Feather here; but whatever happens we mustn't let him know about Nanny."

Sean was a thorn in their sides. As regularly as winter he cast a cold shadow over their lives; but he had learned to be wary, too. He was reminded, every time he looked in a mirror, that bullying could carry unexpected and unpleasant rewards. During the last encounter, when the gang of five had started their wildlife park, Sean was left with a broken nose from the recoil of a heavy calibre hunting rifle.

As they approached him, still pushing the feed sack on the pram wheels, they could see the twist his nose had carried ever since.

They tried to ignore him, but he wouldn't have it. He strolled menacingly into their path as they passed. He was a year older than Jamie and a lot heavier, despite Jamie's unusual height for his fourteen years.

"You look like a bunch o' gippos who've been nickin' stuff off the tip,' scoffed Sean. The pram wheels came to a halt in front of him. "So what's goin' on now, then, eh? Another little plot? Some other con, eh?"

He looked down at the feed sack. The label was face down, and the bare surface gave no clues.

He grinned maliciously. "I'm gonna find out anyway. Might as well tell me now."

Jamie sighed wearily. "Look Sean, we don't bother you; why don't you drop it. Find something else to do. You haven't got the guts to do anything – not while Feather's here, anyway."

Sean scowled. "You're forgettin'. I owe you one." He pointed to his own nose, bent out of shape.

"That was your own fault and you know it," said Emily sullenly.

Sean leaned forward, pushing his face into hers. Before he could reply Feather's growl grew thick and ugly. Sean stepped back a pace. He shrugged.

"Suit yourself . . . just a bunch of gippos," they heard him mutter as he turned and swaggered away.

They pushed on with the pram wheels, eager to get away as fast as possible. They rounded the corner into the lane which led to the side gate, and hurried into the garden.

Harry breathed a heavy sigh of relief. "Close," he said.

"I don't know what you sound so relieved about," said Lara. "He'll keep nosing around now until he finds out what we *are* doing. I bet you."

"We'll just have to keep out of his way, hope he gets bored. Not much else we can do," said Emily.

Nanny improved. With grinning delight they watched the changes daily. She slowly grew more alive, more interested, and hungrier! Flesh formed under the dry, scurfed skin. The knobs and ridges and sharp angles of bone softened and sank as Nanny's body filled and fattened. The scurf receded and the harsh, brittle hair softened and shone as they stroked and groomed her and gave her their constant attention through one long day into the next.

The driver peered down at the pinched, stubbly face of the Weasel. "I remember you. You're the uncle of those kids. The ones with the big dog." The Weasel's eyes gleamed with poisonous satisfaction. "Ah, remember 'em do you?"

"Blimey! How could you forget a dog like that?"

The Weasel grasped the sides of the doorway and hauled himself aboard, trailing the bandaged foot. "Right then, you'll be able to show me where they got off, won't you."

The doors sighed to a close and the bus growled forward, gathering speed down the long, narrow lane.

The children found it hard to tell their parents about Nanny, but Jeff Anderson insisted. For nearly two weeks he came daily, confirming Nanny's progress, asking the same question: do your parents know?

Sheepishly they shook their heads. With a sigh of exasperation he banged down his case. There was an old packing crate lying in a corner of the shed; he dragged it over to where Nanny was

52

busily stripping leaves from a chestnut branch hanging from the ceiling, and sat on it.

"Right. You go and get them and *I'll* tell them."

They shuffled their feet. Jeff stroked Nanny's long ears. His eyes scanned the goat's obviously improving health. "You're worrying too much. When I tell them what you've achieved, they'll give you a medal."

Silently, reluctantly, they straggled out.

It wasn't as bad as they imagined. The five parents (Jamie and Ellen lived only with their mother, their father lived abroad), filed along the narrow paths, fully of curiosity. The children introduced Jeff to their parents, and Jeff introduced the parents to Nanny.

As he had predicted, they were delighted.

"I thought something awful must have happened," cried Jamie and Ellen's mother. "She's so pretty! Has she got a name?"

They told her. Emily's father, keenly aware of his daughter's unbridled enthusiasm – the kind which led her constantly into trouble – said with a hint of suspicion, "What's it doing here?"

"We found her," lied Emily, looking at Jeff. He raised his eyebrows but said nothing. "She must've wandered into the garden at night. You should have seen her . . . "

Jeff explained how near to death Nanny had been. "Look at her now," he said. "You should be very proud of your children. They've done a job even a vet couldn't do. They've brought her back to life with love and constant care, I'm afraid vets often don't have enough time for that."

"And what's more," declared Ellen, tugging her mother's arm. "She's going to have a baby!"

That was the clincher.

"But hadn't we better see if we can find out who's lost her," asked Lara and Harry's mother.

"I'll – er – I'll make some enquiries, but she must have come from miles away. Could be we'll never know," said Jeff, turning away hastily and winking privately to the children as he did so. He excused himself, leaving the three families to enjoy their new pet.

"I shan't be back until next week," he said. "Nanny doesn't need a daily visit now. She's getting everything any goat could possibly need."

"Jeff . . ." began Lara, hesitating.

"Well?"

"As she's doing so well . . . do you think the kid will be all right, too?"

He shook his head thoughtfully. "It's impossible to say. Maybe . . . probably. I don't know. It's a risk, and you have to be prepared for it. I don't want you to be disappointed.

There's a few weeks yet. Enjoy her, help her. The kid will be a bonus – if it survives. I'm sorry if that sounds a bit brutal, but it's better that you face the possibilities."

She smiled, a little sadly. He gave her arm a friendly squeeze and left.

Their lives fell into a routine, with Nanny at the centre. Every morning before school they were out early to change her bedding and water and to lead her into some part of the garden where they could tether her within reach of a banquet of greenery. They watched with amazement as the clear areas began to grow, and the wilderness receded visibly before the onslaught of Nanny's ever-working jaws.

She grew fat and shone, and her indifference fell from her. Any fear of humans she might have had evaporated under a soothing blanket of petting and stroking.

She liked to play butting games (for goats, though like sheep in many ways, are bolder and more fun). She and Feather danced and chased, him yapping, her bleating. Nanny would rise up on her hind legs and box him with her cloven hoofs, a game that was treated with scorn by the dignified Scab. When Nanny came too close Scab raged at her with unsheathed claws and spitting jaws. It didn't stop Nanny, though.

While they were at school the parents took turns to make regular visits into the garden wilderness to check on Nanny's welfare. The goat was always delighted to see them, trotting to the end of her tether, nuzzling one hand while the other stroked her silken ears.

And when the children returned from school they released Nanny from the tether and she followed them everywhere, in all their games. She even climbed the stairs to Lara's bedroom

– until her mother found goat droppings on the carpet and declared the house out of bounds.

Jeff continued to pay a weekly call, and earned their undying gratitude by opening an account for them at the feed merchant, in his own name, so they could keep feeding the balanced diet Nanny needed.

And all the time Sean watched them. They went

to the same school as Sean (though Ellen was in the junior section). He quizzed their friends aggressively for information, but they had none. The five had agreed to keep Nanny a secret from outsiders until after the kid was born. They feared too much attention might set back her improving health.

So Sean watched. He knew the answer was

in the garden, but it seemed there was never a time when the others were not there, too. And he feared Feather – and Scab; their paths had crossed before.

He continued to watch and to wait, and one weekend they gave him his chance. They ran out of the oatmeal mixture from the feed merchant.

"With the pram wheels two can handle it. We don't all have to go," said Emily.

She pulled five grass stems, cut two of them short, and held them bunched in her hands. "Short straws get the job!"

Harry and Ellen drew them out.

"Aw, not her," wailed Harry. "That's not fair."

Ellen flounced indignantly. "I'm as good as you any day!"

He groaned; the others grinned. "Maybe one of us should go, too," said Jamie. "To look after Harry."

The younger boy blushed hotly. "Come on," he muttered to Ellen, turning on his heel. "Just don't go on, that's all."

Sean, who by chance was turning into the street at the far end, saw them go. Harry was setting a stiff pace, pulling the wheels by a length of rope they had fastened in a loop to the front. Ellen ran along behind trying to hop aboard. "It won't hurt you," Sean heard her complain. "I'm only light . . ."

They turned a corner out of sight and he hurried after them, following always just one corner behind, until they reached the feed merchant.

He hid until they reappeared with a sack loaded on the pram wheels; then he swaggered into the feed merchant's warehouse. A few innocent questions soon told him what he wanted to know. He flew after Harry and Ellen, triumph in his malicious grin.

They were waiting at a crossing on the main road when he saw them. They didn't notice him.

"After this old truck. Get ready. Be careful or you'll tip it off," said Harry, turning his attention to the sack as the battered truck clattered by.

It passed them, slowing as it did so, pulling into the roadside. It stopped there, engine running. One brake light was smashed but the other shone red.

Harry and Ellen crossed the road, nursing the sack. The truck coughed to silence. They trudged on, arguing as they went. They never noticed the vehicle. The flat bed of its open back was twisted and heeling on broken springs. An oily mess of rags, bits of twisted metal, and frayed rope littered the back of it; bits of cardboard lay in a soggy, oily goo.

In the cab the Weasel's lips compressed into a grim line. He reached softly across the torn seats and gripped a length of timber lying beside him. His other hand grasped the door handle.

Before he could move he heard a voice call. "Here! Wait up you!"

The Weasel stopped. Harry and Ellen were ahead of the truck now, looking back. They never noticed him in the cab and the truck meant nothing to them. Instead their wide eyes were fixed on Sean sprinting towards them from the crossing.

Their faces paled. Sean towered over them, panting from the run, face full of glee. "So," he scoffed. "Been getting the dinner, have we? Sort of muck pigs like you would eat." He put one foot on the sack. "Pigs and *goats*!"

As he spat the word he shoved hard with his heel. It tore through the paper sack and the powdered grain leaked in a little heap on to the pavement.

Harry and Ellen could think of nothing to say. They tried desperately not to show their fear. Sean snorted. "You tell Jimmy-the-one I'll be round. I wanna see which one smells worse – him, or his new friend."

With that he shoved again at the sack with his foot. The wheels overbalanced and the sack fell off, spilling its contents across the pavement. Sean swaggered off in the direction the children had been walking, whistling through his teeth.

They managed to haul the sack back on to the wheels, spilling more of the contents. By the time it was on board half the grain was scattered over the pavement.

They were too busy to notice the old truck start up again. It idled along the kerbside, its shadow falling on them as they struggled, and continued past until it was level with Sean.

The window lowered and the Weasel called out to Sean, "Hey, you. Friends of yours, are they?"

For a moment Sean was scarlet with guilt, until the Weasel said, "They better not be, if you know what's good for you."

Sean's face changed to an obsequious grin, in which he managed to express a little of his truculent hostility. "No chance. I owe 'em more yet."

The truck door opened. "Get in. Maybe we can do each other a favour."

Harry and Ellen struggled back with their load, trailing a fine trickle of grain as they went. By the time they reported to the others Sean was already climbing from the truck outside his home on one of the nearby estates.

The Weasel was saying, "I wanna hear everythin', mind. You keep me in touch. I'll think up a few surprises for 'em."

His hand appeared through the truck window, with money folded between the fingers. Sean took the money, nodding, and stuffed it in his back pocket.

Five

Nanny belonged to them all, and yet they all recognized she would always be most precious to Lara. There was no special reason. Just as dogs – and, of course, Feather – would always be favourite with Jamie, and Scab would retain a special place in Emily's thoughts, so Lara's heart could always be guaranteed to melt when she watched the soft-nosed, sad-eyed Nanny.

Not that she *was* sad. Nanny became a comic character. She stood on her hind legs and reached far up to eat the succulent leaves on the lower branches of trees; she nosed into pockets. Once she even tried to eat the washing; another time they found her in the branches of a shrub, agile as a cat.

But Nanny could also look sadly down her Roman nose as if part of her still dwelt in the unhappy days of her cruel past. It was that darkly-hidden part of Nanny's mind, which could never be reached, that pained Lara so. She knew goats could not remember like people; but Lara could imagine the months of lonely pain embodied in the sight that met her eyes when she had entered the Weasel's appalling shed.

The only times Lara spent away from Nanny were when she was forbidden, by school, by home chores, or by meals. Sometimes even her meals were shared with the goat and its swelling, ripening pregnancy. Nanny would watch, head cocked, while Lara ate a sandwich, constantly ducking aside to protect her lunch from the goat's inquiring nose. She talked to her about her friends, her school, her homework, her plans . . . while Nanny gently chewed the cud or bleated a sad, companionable reply.

So it was to be expected that Lara would be the first to notice the change in Nanny's behaviour: a restlessness, a desire to hide herself in secluded corners of the garden away from Feather's playfulness and the children's constant chatter.

They all stood sombrely in a semi-circle round Nanny as Jeff checked her over. He stroked her wide, plump flank.

"Well, it's a bit of a guess, because we don't know when she first conceived," he said. "But I don't reckon there's more than a week to go before she has the kid."

Harry and Emily linked hands and danced round the clearing. Lara hugged Nanny and Jamie grinned sheepishly. Ellen said, "But where will it come *from*?"

Jeff grinned. "You'll see soon enough." His face became serious. "Look, wouldn't you rather I took Nanny back to the surgery and cared for her there until after she's had the kid?"

Harry, Emily and Lara spun round to face him. Jamie and Ellen stared open-mouthed.

"No way," cried Emily. "She's one of us now. We've been waiting so long we feel like *we're* giving birth. Not a chance."

She looked at Lara. "He doesn't trust us."

Jeff said hastily, still serious, "No, it's not that. It's just . . . well, I warned you - about the kid, remember?

"There's no knowing if it's going to be okay – it probably will be," he added hastily, watching their gaping faces, "I can hear its heartbeat well enough with the stethoscope.

"But some damage might have been done before you rescued her. If there's anything wrong . . . I don't want you to be distressed."

"The kid must be all right," said Lara firmly. "After what Nanny's been through it would be too unfair otherwise."

She saw Jeff start to speak and pressed on, "Oh I know life's not like that. But I have a feeling about it. It *is* going to be all right. And anyway, if something is going to go wrong, she'll need to be with us. She means a lot to us, and I think we mean a lot to her, too."

Jeff smiled. "I guess I knew what you'd say. And I'll be here, too. That's a promise.

"Keep an eye on her. If you notice her behaving

oddly, ring me. Day or night, it doesn't matter. She might bleat a lot, or maybe just keep trying to find a way to lie comfortably. And her udder will get much harder just before the birth, as it fills with milk. If you're in any doubt, telephone. I'd rather come a dozen times than risk not being here."

"What about when we're at school?" said Harry.

"We'll get our mums to look out," said Emily. "They're about as excited over this as we are. We'll organize a roster. They can Nanny-sit for an hour each in turn til we get home. It's only for a week, after all."

A sharp intake of breath from Ellen made them all turn. She was standing wide-eyed, her hand to her mouth. "We still don't know how to milk. We didn't think we needed to yet."

They all looked at Jeff. He frowned, thinking. "Mmmm, tell you what. Get some rubber gloves. You know, washing up gloves, and make a pin prick in the longest finger. Fill them with water and one can hold while one tries to milk the finger."

They all laughed.

"No, I'm serious. Sounds silly, but I can't think of anything better – and it might help."

Once Jeff had gone they begged the rubber gloves from their parents and experimented. In minutes they were helpless, giggling on the floor while Feather nosed playfully from one to the other. Scab sniffed the discarded, leaking gloves and walked huffily away.

"It's a good job we've got a week," groaned Jamie.

It wasn't a week, it was nine days, but no one minded because it was a Sunday and they were all there.

Dismissing all her parents' concerns, Lara moved a camp-bed into the shed and slept the Saturday night next to Nanny, with a torch beside her. She promised the others she would wake them if anything happened. At seven on Sunday morning her mother brought her a flask of tea. Lara was sitting on the edge of the camp-bed, studying Nanny.

Her mother poured the tea. "Everything all right?"

"I'm not sure. She woke up about an hour ago, and she hasn't settled since. She keeps coming over and poking her nose in my ear."

Her mother produced some biscuits from her pocket and gave them to Lara. "Maybe she's just not used to you being here."

Lara shook her head thoughtfully as Nanny turned a complete circle in a corner of the shed, made to lie down, stood, and turned again.

Lara was decided. "No. This is it. I'm sure of it. She knows, too."

She walked over to the goat and reached down to feel her udder. "I'm sure it's got harder. Not much but —" She turned to her mother. "Would you call Jeff?"

Her mother nodded, concerned. "It seems a bit early to be worrying him . . . "

"He said anytime. Please Mum. And tell the others, too."

Her mother smiled. She left the flask with Lara and opened the shed door. "I'll tell them straight away. Will you be all right til I get back?"

Lara nodded and her mother left. After a second or two Lara suddenly ran over to the door and threw it open. "But ring Jeff *first*," she called.

He arrived half an hour later. By then everyone had gathered at the shed: the five children and their parents. There wasn't room inside for all of them so the parents waited outside while Jeff and the children gathered round Nanny.

Jeff nursed the long silky ears. He nudged Lara, who looked deeply worried, and said lightly, "Perfect handling. It's definitely going to be this morning. Could take a while, though."

Ellen was listening to them, her face a picture of doubt. "Is the kid really in there?" she said, pointing to Nanny's swollen belly.

Jeff nodded.

"But how's it ever going to get out?" cried Ellen.

The others laughed at her bewilderment. "Wait and see," smiled Jeff.

Nanny was still restless, circling the inside of the shed, pawing at her bedding, nosing at the children. Now and then one of the parents would poke their head inside to see if there were any developments.

"She's so hot," said Emily, feeling Nanny's coat as the goat sat on its side.

Suddenly Nanny's whole frame tensed. Even under her hair they could see the muscles knot along her body and into her neck. She stayed like it for seconds, but it seemed like minutes to the children.

"That's normal," said Jeff. "It's a contraction, like in humans; but it means something's started to happen; we shouldn't have long to wait."

Lara was kneeling at Nanny's head. "Did you hear that," she whispered to the goat. "Not long now."

But Lara was wrong. Two hours later the kid had still not appeared. Nanny's coat was shiny with sweat, the hair stuck down as if someone had thrown a bucket of water over her. Her body was trembling with the constant, compulsive straining of her knotted muscles every few minutes.

Jamie's mother brought everyone coffee and biscuits. Harry, Ellen and Emily were slouched on the shed floor, backs against the wooden walls, Jamie was outside pacing back and forth with Feather, kicking impatiently at bits of stick.

Lara still knelt at Nanny's head, soothing the goat with her quiet voice. Jeff had lifted Nanny's tail, and his hand had disappeared into the orifice beneath: the dilated vulva through which the kid would be born. He looked worried. He withdrew his hand, shaking his head. "As far as I can feel, everything seems okay," he said. "She just doesn't seem to be able to push hard enough – hang on, she's having another go."

They both felt the body harden and the back

67

arch slightly as Nanny's muscles spasmed in contraction.

"Why does she do it if it doesn't work?" said Ellen. "She'll just get tired."

"It's instinct," said Jeff. "She can't help herself from trying to push the kid out. That's how nature works. Poor old Nanny's not really strong enough for this yet. Not after what she's been through."

"Oh yes she is," interrupted Lara. She held the goat's head in both hands and stared into the deep, slotted eyes. "You show him Nanny. Go on – another one's coming; I can feel it – go on Nanny, push . . ."

Jeff lifted her tail, examining the opening as Nanny strained, muscles hard under the skin.

"It's coming!" he cried. "She's done it. Look! Here's the feet and the nose."

The shed went dark as parents crowded through the open door. There was a scuffle as Emily, Harry and Ellen leapt from the floor and pushed closer.

Under the goat's tail five centimetres of nose was sticking out into the morning air. It was slick with a clear, viscous membrane still clinging to it. Under the nose, neat and small as pale fingers, were two cloven hooves.

Emily was frantic with excitement, holding herself tightly under control, conscious of the need not to worry Nanny. "O wow," she hissed, "Look at that. Look at that!"

Harry and Jamie stared, open mouthed, while Jeff felt expertly along Nanny's abdomen. "This next is the hard part," he muttered, almost to himself. "Once the heads's through she'll be okay. Come on old girl, you can do it . . . "

Lara was biting her bottom lip, her cheek down alongside Nanny's muzzle. She couldn't speak. Ellen had slipped her hand into her mother's. Her face was pale and puzzled. She shook her mother's hand until her mother leaned down and Ellen whispered in her ear. "Is that it?"

Her mother nodded, smiling.

"A baby goat?"

"Yes. Isn't it wonderful?"

"Yuk," said Ellen. She thought for a while and added, "Poor Nanny."

Another contraction swept through the goat. This time Jeff had his hands on the little hooves, gently easing them out. As the contraction reached its peak Nanny suddenly shifted a little, bleating. There was a quick, soft gurgling sound and the kid's whole head was exposed to view, glistening wet, with the forelegs tucked under its chin. It gave a small involuntary jerk. Everybody caught their breath. Emily, who was almost inside Jeff's arms in her excitement, said. "It's alive, Lara! It just moved. I saw it."

They couldn't see Lara's face as it slid further down Nanny's neck, her bottom lip raw from the bite of her teeth; her tears flooding in a river down Nanny's coat.

All eyes except Lara's were on the kid. Another spasm passed through Nanny and at it's peak Lara heard the wet "flop" as the newborn goat was ejected, shiny with the foetal membrane, on to the hay-covered floor of the shed. A quiet, reverent cheer of delight went up from the parents. For the first time Lara looked.

For one heart-stopping moment, as she watched the small, damp body lying still on the floor she thought it must be dead. Jeff's gentle hands were clearing the mucus from its nostrils and mouth. Suddenly the kid emitted a tiny, delicate sneeze, and trembled down to its tail.

Lara hugged Nanny until the goat was forced to struggle free from the embrace. "Thank you," she whispered into its neck. "Oh thank you, thank you."

She jumped up, wiping the tears from her face, and Nanny stood, too, turning to nose at the kid. She immediately began the ritual licking of her newborn, methodically cleaning away the wet membrane, leaving the coat spiky as rough grass.

With every lick the kid acquired its natural infant charm. Even the parents were blowing into their handkerchiefs and cooing over the tiny creature.

Lara was talking gently to Nanny. One hand stroked the goat, the other gently stroked the kid. "It's beautiful, Nanny. So beautiful," she murmured.

The kid was a pure, clean white except for one ear, which was a deep, rich black. The line between the two was so precise it looked as if the ear had been sewn on. The hoofs, which had been pale as translucent bone at birth, were already darkening to brown.

Nanny was talking to it, fussing in a conversational way, somewhere between a bleat and a throaty grumble. Suddenly the kid pulled a foreleg out from under it and placed the hoof firmly on the floorboards. The second foreleg followed, trembling violently.

"It's trying to stand up," cried Lara. "Already!" She clutched Emily in excitement and the two stood frozen in tense anticipation, grunting themselves with every effort the kid made.

It was on its front legs, its back angled steeply as it tried to work out what to do with its hindquarters, how to control its new muscles.

A hind leg moved into play and the kid heaved itself up, slipped, and sat down again, puzzled. Nanny nuzzled it, encouraging, urging. The kid began again. "Couldn't we help it," said Lara, biting her fingers to stop them from interfering.

Jeff shook his head. "Best let them get on with it," he said. "It's been going on for thousands of years, don't forget. I'm sure they'll know what to do – look, it's going to make it."

There was a strained silence as the kid wobbled to its feet again. This time the rear hooves stayed in position, trembling fiercely with the effort. The kid tottered a couple of steps before its forelegs slid out from under and its chin hit the ground. With a fine, soft bleat it sat down and began again.

This time the kid made it. Its legs were firmer, stronger, knowing what they had to do. It wobbled erect and stayed there. It tottered a few steps, Nanny always at its side, stopped and bleated. Nanny returned the sound.

The kid's head went down instinctively, nosing under Nanny's chest for a teat. Jeff shook his head, smiling.

"Wrong end, chump," he said affectionately.

He gently steered the kid to the warm, milk-hard udder, guiding the fragile creature to a teat. The kid butted hungrily at the udder, nearly knocking Nanny over. "Hey!" cried Ellen, "Don't be so rough!"

"It's okay," laughed Jeff. "That's instinct, too. That's how the kid gets her to let the milk go."

The kid had engaged a teat, and as it sucked hungrily its tiny stump of a tail thrashed the air. Everyone laughed in soft delight.

Jeff said, "By the way. It's a girl, if you hadn't noticed. Another Nanny. What are you going to call it?" He put a hand on Lara's shoulder.

"It's the best Sunday I've ever had," said Lara, grinning up at him. "I think we should call it Sunday."

No one argued. Spontaneously she flung her arms round Jeff's neck, dragging him down to where she could plant a kiss on his cheek. He chortled with surprise and Lara blushed, suddenly shy. "Thank you," she said softly, "for everything."

"I didn't do anything," said Jeff. "I wouldn't have believed it *could* be done if you hadn't shown me. Nanny's the one who should get the credit. Nanny . . . and you lot."

Six

The days that followed were the best they could remember.

In the beginning they sat one either side of Nanny and milked a teat each. Nanny, unused to milking, would try to walk away, stepping in the buckets and capsizing them, filling their shoes with warm milk. Those who were not milking fell helpless with delight into the sweet-smelling hay of Nanny's bed – until it was their turn.

Scab, who had shunned all the previous excitement as beneath his dignity, was now ingratiating himself on everyone with his pleas for milk. They soon learned the trick of squirting the milk sideways from the teats in a fine white thread which Feather and Scab would both catch in their mouths.

Sunday, with Nanny, was the five friends' constant companion. She was soon as playful as Feather. She quickly discovered Scab was different: aloof, dangerous even; and Scab learned that a nanny goat will charge even a scabby old tom-cat to protect its young.

Nanny was weakened considerably by the birth of Sunday, but with extra vitamins, a concentrated diet, and all she could eat from the endless foliage of the garden, she recovered quickly. She and Sunday spent their days content together in the garden while the five children were at school.

Their mothers kept an eye out for the goats. Nanny was tethered on a long rope but there was no reason to tether Sunday, who was glued to Nanny at all times – usually to a teat. The growing kid's head would butt at the udder, her tiny bud of a tail wriggling with pleasure.

Once Sunday had been born the secret was too much to keep. The whole neighbourhood learned of it next morning at school. That same evening – for a modest payment – they were admitted in ones and twos to admire the wobbling, one-day-old, Sunday.

As the kid grew older, so the visitors increased. The garden filled with the delighted squeals of visiting children. Emily was making money.

The more adventurous sat either side of Nanny twice a day, morning and evening, after Sunday had drunk her fill, and learned to milk. They paid for the privilege. They paid, too, to help clean out the bedding in the shed, to groom the mother and her kid, to find and hang fresh bunches of succulent leaves.

"I can't believe it," said Emily. "They're even paying to work!"

They sold the excess milk to their parents at inflated prices and gradually the two goats became not only a constant source of pleasure, but a small source of income for the five friends, too.

The goats' reputation spread far around the neighbourhood. School afternoons ended in a race to reach home before the visitors, who were all eager to groom and clean and milk, and to pay for the pleasure.

The pocket money was fun, as a side-line, but neither Emily nor the others were bothered whether people came. Sometimes they found the visitors a nuisance because they cut down the time the five could spend alone with the goats. But the visitors turned out to be a good thing. Without them they might have lost Sunday forever.

They arrived home on a Friday afternoon after school, dumped their bags in their respective homes and ran out to Nanny and Sunday.

Nanny was there, bleating a greeting on the end of her tether. Emily's mother was there, too, with Lara and Harry's mother; and Feather bounced over to greet them.

But there was no sign of Sunday.

"We can't find her anywhere," said Emily's mother. "We've been all round."

At first none of them were too concerned. Sunday had a habit of finding small, shaded corners in which she would curl, safely sheltered, and sleep. They knew now where most of these corners were.

Jamie raised his eyebrows. "She's probably under the old lavender bush. I'll have a look."

Lara's mother shook her head. "We already did, and behind the old hedge. We even braved the big patch of nettles – I got stung. There's no sign of her."

"When was the last time you saw her?" asked Emily, a crop of worry lines beginning to crease her forehead.

Her mother shrugged. "That's the trouble. I'm not certain. I poked my head out a couple of times and saw Nanny. I sort of assumed Sunday would be here somewhere. I don't think I've seen her all afternoon."

The children gasped.

"Maybe she went for a walk," said Ellen brightly.

"Not without Nanny," insisted Lara. "There's no way she'd even dream of it.

"Spread out. We've got to cover the whole garden; the smallest places. She's still only tiny remember."

They called and ferreted into corners they had never seen before, but they were greeted only with silence, or the clatter of disturbed pigeons overhead.

They met back at the clearing by the shed, all flushed and panting, the sharp bite of panic nipping at their thoughts. In some instinctive way the panic had transmitted itself to Nanny. The goat was pacing the undergrowth, calling, searching, growing gradually more restless.

"We'd better call the police and report her missing," said Emily's mother.

"No!" replied Jamie sharply. He was afraid the police might ask too many questions about where she came from. They had to handle this themselves.

Three school friends sauntered into the clearing, the first of those who came every evening to help care for the goats.

"Good. That's eight of us. Ten with you two." Jamie indicated the two mothers.

"We'll pair off and search the roads. I'm certain she's not here and even if she is, she'll be all right while Nanny's here."

He sent two searching in the direction of the shops, two down to the Riverdale estate, Lara and Emily headed towards the school.

The two mothers took Ellen with them in the direction of the main road while Jamie risked the wrath of neighbours in all the nearby streets as he stealthily checked gardens, back and front.

Harry and a school friend were the last to return more than an hour later. They had scoured the distant Riverdale estate and they were tired and empty-handed.

"No one's even seen her – and we saw loads of people from school," he said. "They promised to keep their eyes open."

They flopped to the grass with the others, all exhausted from the search.

Nanny was bleating plaintively. She hadn't been milked and the pressure on her udder was reminding her of the absence of her kid.

Lara hugged her neck. "We have to do something," she said. "We can't just leave it – if we have to tell the police then I think we'd better do it soon, before it's dark."

A silence settled over them all.

"I vote we call them," said Emily. "I don't see we've got any choice."

One by one the others nodded. "Let's go," she said, getting up and heading for the house.

The noise of them crushing twigs and grass as they filed after her smothered the sound of the ringing telephone until they were quite close. Emily, leading the way, heard it first. She flew to answer it. She was already hanging up when the others finally panted in around her.

"Thanks a lot," she was calling excitedly into the telephone. "Just keep an eye on her. Don't go near her; she might take fright and run off."

She hung up, turning to the others. "That was Shelly, one of the twins who comes to help sometimes after school. She's seen Sunday – down at the river, near the weir."

Everyone gasped in horror.

"That must be more than a mile away!" said Lara, shocked. "How could she have found her way down there?"

Jamie was already heading for the door. "Don't know, but we'd better get down there. If she finds her way on to the bridge she'll be in trouble.

"Bring Nanny," he yelled over his shoulder.

People had drowned at the weir. The water plunged in a furious torrent of brown, boiling

78

spume to the lower level, where it churned in a frothing rage from which its victims had little hope of escape.

Lara and Emily's mothers were the last to arrive at the river's edge. They looked down from the parkland which bordered the river.

Sunday was trembling in the centre of the weir bridge, a fine spray from the plummeting waters curling at her legs.

"Oh my God," murmured Lara's mother.

They could see Nanny straining to climb on the bridge, tugging against the lead which Jamie held in his grasp. The other four children were gathered round him. The women ran forward, calling as they did so, but their yells were lost in the blanketing roar of the weir waters.

Jamie moved on to the bridge. Nanny was ahead of him still tugging at the leash.

"Jamie!" yelled Emily's mother. No one could hear. The women reached the weir and shoved past the children. Jamie was already out on the bridge. One hand gripped the rail; the other gripped the leash with Nanny bleating and straining at its end.

"You shouldn't have let him go," wailed Emily's mother. "He'll get himself killed."

They all watched, frozen with suspense as Jamie moved forward. Sunday had been facing away from them, not hearing Nanny bleat over the roar of the river, but as Jamie and Nanny edged on to the bridge she sensed their steps through the old boards and she turned.

79

At the bank the group caught their breath as the tiny figure swung round on the narrow walkway, and skipped back to its mother, bleating with delight.

Sunday was nearly there when her hooves skidded on a wet plank and she sprawled, sliding forward. A volley of screams rent the air, tearing a hole in the blanketing roar of the water. Sunday

recovered, climbed to her feet and trotted forward more carefully until she was nose to nose with Nanny. She began to edge past her.

Lara's eyes opened wide with horror and she yelled, "If Nanny tries to turn she'll knock Sunday in!"

Her shout was drowned by the thunder of the weir. Nanny was already twisting against the restraint of the leash, looking for a way to turn, not finding it. She began to panic.

There was nothing Jamie could do. He let go. The leash swept the boards as Nanny nuzzled at her kid. Sunday was nosing along Nanny's flank, searching for her teats.

"Oh no," cried out Lara. "Not there; not there . . ."

Nanny began to back along the weir bridge. From the bank they called encouragement to her, but the noise only served to confuse her. She reared on her hind legs, away from the handrail, attempting to swing her body round on the narrow platform. There was no room.

She reared again, this time the other way. For a moment her front hooves rested lightly on the metal handrail. Next second she had dropped to the boards once more, this time facing back to the bank.

She trotted neatly off the weir bridge, Sunday chasing after the milk smell from Nanny's fat, warm udder.

The children all cheered. Jamie blushed with embarrassed pride as they congratulated him.

The two women stood silently by, their grim and angry faces contradicting their relief in a way which only parents understand.

Lara's mother pointed straight-armed back through the park. "Get those animals home," she rapped. "If this ever happens again they're going."

She turned to Jamie. "Are you out of your head?

81

Do you know what would have happened if you'd fallen in there?"

Jamie nodded sheepishly. Lara flew to his aid. "What were we supposed to do – leave her out there on her own?"

"Don't answer me back, young lady."

She turned to Jamie again. "You've taken years off my life. God knows what your mother will say." She pointed firmly up the slope of the park. "Go."

Heads down, Lara leading Nanny while the kid sucked clumsily behind, the dejected group trudged home. By the time they reached the garden the two women had softened.

As they threaded their way to the shed clearing Lara was insisting, "But I don't believe she'd wander all that way without Nanny. I just don't. Something's going on."

Her mother shrugged "Well, she didn't fly. Maybe she was looking for water or something; animals do that kind of thing – oh!"

She cannoned into Harry and Ellen, who had stopped behind Jamie. He had his hands on his hips and he was staring at the shed.

Emblazoned across the front in vivid red aerosol letters a metre high was the word *Gippos*. The paint swept across the door, which was swinging open, and smothered the window.

"I knew it," breathed Lara grimly.

The inside of the shed was worse. The smell of cellulose paint hung in the air. Yellow and green and red obscenities had been sprayed over everything, so that the evening sunlight seemed to carry the tinge of colours.

The hanging bundle of food was sprayed, and the milking bucket and the sack of oats; Nanny's hay bed, grooming brushes, even the inside of the roof. All the contents of the shed had been hurled into a paint-stained confusion.

The children stood in the doorway silently surveying the mess. The two mothers were outraged.

"Who did it?" stormed Emily's mother, her anger with the children forgotten. "How dare they! It's vandalism; nothing else. Did they think it was funny? I'm calling the police."

Emily grabbed her before she stormed away. "Don't fuss. The police can't do anything about it. We don't even know who did it."

"It's *not* staying like that," snapped Emily's mother firmly. "You can fix it yourself, or find out who did it, but we're not letting it rest!"

The two women swept away, fuming.

The children turned back to the shed. Emily wearily picked up the overturned, sprayed milking bucket and threw the brushes into it. "It stinks of paint in here. We can't let them back in until we've scrubbed it out a bit."

Jamie's jaw was working in silent fury. "We don't have to take this," he muttered. "I don't care how big he is, we'll have it out with him at school tomorrow."

"We don't know it *was* Sean," offered Lara, uncertainly.

"No?" snapped Jamie. "Who was it called us

gippos the other day? Who else do you know who's poisonous enough to do a thing like this?"

"But I can't believe he'd deliberately leave Sunday on the weir like that. Maybe he just took her off somewhere so he could get in here, and she wandered down there on her own."

"Does it make any difference? One slip and she would have been just as dead – and it would have

been his fault. He's got to pay. Somehow he's *got* to pay."

"Well it's no good us falling out over it," said Emily. "Maybe he'll give it a rest now he's had his revenge. Come on; let's clean it up. The place needed painting anyway. We can buy some paint tomorrow after school. What colour d'you reckon?"

Seven

They didn't paint the shed next day. Nor did
Jamie confront Sean at school.

Sean wasn't there. Jamie searched for him at
morning break and lunchtime, but there was no
sign of him. He saw Lara at the beginning of
afternoon school. "I don't trust him," muttered
Jamie. "He's up to something."

"Could be sick . . ." suggested Lara.

Jamie nodded. "In the head. He wasn't sick
when he sprayed the shed yesterday, was he?"

Lara tried to lighten the mood. "Maybe he
poisoned himself with paint fumes," she smiled.

Jamie's brow furrowed. He stalked off irritably
to his classes.

Lara's flippant responses had failed to suppress
the nagging worry which gnawed at her mind.

Sean had the whole day to do as he pleased,
while they were stuck until the end of school . . .

Lara looked at her watch. Two hours before

home time. She knew she wouldn't be able to concentrate on anything all afternoon.

When it was over they ran home at a trot. Ellen moaned because they were going too fast, but they didn't slow down.

Both Nanny and Sunday were gone.

The children ran desperately from path to path, calling, but they knew in their hearts they would not find either animal in the garden. A growing panic overwhelmed them.

They raced back to the houses. "When was the last time anyone checked on Nanny?" gasped Lara, bursting in on her mother in the kitchen.

Her mother caught Lara's mood. "About an hour ago," she replied, alarmed. "Why? What's happened?"

"They've gone. Both of them." Tears were beginning to break through Lara's faltering composure as she turned back out of the kitchen to join the others. Her mother followed, her face fully of worry.

"I'm going to check up and down the road," said Lara. "Maybe someone's seen them." She ran off.

The others, mothers included, split up and combed the garden. There was no sign of the goats. They widened their search out into the street. Lara was on her way back, running along the pavement with a straggle of children behind her.

"I picked them up as I went. They were on their way here to help with the milking," panted Lara. "They're going to help us look. We'll have to split into groups; get organized."

A voice called from across the street "Hey!"

A young head was framed in an open upstairs window in one of the estate houses opposite.

"That's Jason Potter," said Harry. "He's in my class. Been off a couple of weeks with chicken pox."

"What you looking for?" called Jason.

"We've lost the goats," yelled Harry.

Jason pointed along the road towards the city. "A truck picked 'em up. 'Bout forty-five minutes ago. I saw 'em."

They all tore across the road so they could hear him more easily. "What do you mean, a truck?" said Jamie tersely.

"A truck . . . just a truck; two guys in a truck, with writing on the side."

"What did it say?"

"I dunno, didn't think about it really. Ask Sean. He might know."

There was a brief silence. The five felt a fluttering sickness as their stomachs dropped suddenly into a bottomless hole.

"Sean?" echoed Lara, wrapping her arms round herself to stop the shivering.

"He was here, too. I think he was waiting for them when they drew up."

"Did he go with them?"

"No. He walked off in that direction." Jason pointed along the street.

Lara turned to Jamie. "We have to find him. It's the only chance."

He nodded. The whole group set off at a run in

87

the direction Jason had indicated. On the way they collected other children who were playing in their gardens, or in the street. The crowd grew until it was thick and furious as a bee swarm.

Most of them knew Sean. One child reported seeing him turn towards the local shopping centre. With a whoop the crowd chased after.

"There he is," someone yelled.

Ahead they saw Sean's back as he swaggered on, his fingers thrust into his jeans pockets, his thumbs outside, snagged in his belt. A hissing whistle drifted tunelessly from between his teeth. He heard the running feet behind him and turned. At first he didn't realize the crowd was chasing after him, and when he did it was too late to get out of sight.

In any case, daunting as they looked, his pride would not allow him to bolt. He stood his ground, a sneer on his face. He spotted first Jamie, then Feather running with the crowd, and his face grew surly. The crowd slowed, gasping, to a halt.

"Got a problem, Jimmy-the-one?" said Sean to Jamie.

"Where's Nanny?" panted Jamie. "And Sunday?"

"How would I know? You're the one who likes the stink of goats."

"Two men took them. In a truck. And you helped. You helped steal them. If you don't tell us we'll get the police."

Sean's face lit up with triumph. "Oh yeah? Well why don't you do just that, dozo? I'll tell you why. Because you stole 'em yourself. From the Weasel."

He saw the stunned look on the faces of the five friends. They had no idea Sean knew so much. And if Sean knew the Weasel, then the Weasel must know where they lived, where the goats were. The incident the previous day began to fall into place.

"He was banned from keeping animals," shouted Emily angrily. "You had no right! Not you or the Weasel!"

"He's not keeping 'em," scowled Sean, "He's selling 'em."

"Who to?"

"None of your business. Hey –!"

He was suddenly cut short as Jamie flew at him. The younger boy had tangled with Sean before and come off worse, but Jamie's fury smothered his sense of caution. He lunged at Sean and the two boys fell to the floor flailing at each other.

Feather hurled himself snarling into the mêlée, uncertain where to bite. Harry got his hands on the dog's collar and held him back. The two boys were rolling and punching in a small pocket of space in the centre of the crowd.

When the struggling died away Jamie was kneeling astride Sean's chest. A sleeve was ripped almost entirely from Jamie's white school shirt, blood and dirt streaked the back of it. His knees were pinning the bigger boy's arms to the floor. A small admiring cheer went up from the crowd. No one had ever seen Sean beaten before. Feather snarled quietly, restrained by Harry.

Jamie snarled, too, his face pinched with rage, his fist raised menacingly.

"Where'd they go?" he demanded. "Tell me or I'll—"

For a moment Sean's eyes were filled with fear as he gazed up at the raised fist and the ring of faces that surrounded him. But his features twisted into a grin as he studied Jamie's face and realized he was safe. Jamie, he sensed, would never hit him in cold blood.

"Get stuffed," he spat. "You wouldn't have the guts."

Lara stepped into his view. "Please, Sean." Her face was desperate. "Please tell us. I'll give you anything. Nanny would have died if we hadn't taken her. The Weasel was just starving her to death. It was awful. You wouldn't . . . you couldn't—"

She stopped, unable to go on without her face crumpling into tears.

"Aaagh," scowled Sean. "Do me a favour; it's just a goat. That's all."

He paused. "Anyway, I don't know where they took 'em. No idea. They didn't tell me. I just had to show where to find them."

He stared up at the hostile faces that studied him contemptuously. Jamie lifted himself wearily from Sean's prone body. The bigger boy scrambled to his feet, careful to keep his distance from Feather.

All around him faces stared silently.

"No good looking at me like that," he snapped. "They stole it; from the Weasel. He had a right to get it back. It was his."

"That's not true!" yelled Emily hotly. "He's been banned. For cruelty. He shouldn't have had them!"

"The truck," said Jamie, desperately. "What was it like?"

Sean shrugged. "I dunno. Didn't look, really."

Jamie yelled at him, "Think, for God's sake!"

Sean was learning a new respect for the angry Jamie. "How the hell would I know," he said moodily. "Abbey, or Abbot; somethin' like that. I remember that on account of it sounding like it was to do with churches."

He grinned humourlessly. "Bet it wasn't, though; not judgin' from the guys who were in it."

The words hung in the air as the crowd turned them over in their minds . . . abbey, abbot. A few people shrugged. Lara was frowning. The words danced in her thoughts. The letters seemed to rearrange themselves in her head, rattling like bones against one another.

Suddenly she felt the cold grip of a new fear. She turned to the crowd. "Who's got a pencil. Quick. Anyone?"

"I've got a biro," called a small boy. He passed it to Lara. Everyone watched silently while she wrote carefully on the palm of her hand. She thrust her hand under Sean's nose. "Is that the word?"

"Yeah," he said. "I remember now. How come you guessed that? What's it mean anyway?"

Lara showed her hand to Jamie. Written across the palm was *abbatoir*. She choked, trembling over the words as she said, for everyone to hear, "It comes from French. It means slaughterhouse. Where they kill animals for meat."

She looked at Sean and her eyes were filled with hatred and despair.

"I didn't know," he blustered. "You can't blame me." He looked around him. Every face studied him with contempt. "This lot stole it anyway," he said, looking from face to face. "They had no right . . ."

Jamie wasn't listening. He had spotted a telephone box on the far side of the road.

"Who's got some change? For the telephone," he asked.

Hands fished in pockets and dropped a fistful of coins into his palm. He raced across the road and into the box, followed by the rest of the crowd, leaving Sean scowling alone. He thrust his hands in his pockets and stamped angrily away.

"What do we do now?" Emily asked Jamie. She watched as he flicked through the telephone directory.

"Vet," muttered Jamie. "Vet, veterinary, veterinary surgeons."

His finger was moving down the page. "We've got to get hold of Jeff. He'll help – if we're not too late.

"Got it!" he cried. He dropped the coins into the machine and punched out the digits.

An interminable wait followed. The crowd thronged round the box, all straining to hear.

"Hello," said Jamie. "Can I speak to Mr

Anderson?" There was a pause. "But it's urgent. Really. It's desperate."

Another pause. "I don't care. He must come to the phone. Now. Please get him. Tell him it's Jamie – about the goats. Tell him that," he added.

Silence fell over the crowd. The clang of more coins dropping into the machine disturbed the quiet briefly, and everybody fell to waiting.

Suddenly Jamie blurted, "Jeff? Jeff, it's Jamie. Someone's taken the goats. Both of them."

The crowd listened in silence as Jamie explained what had happened and answered the questions Jeff put to him. Finally Jamie hung up and stepped from the box. "He said to wait here. He's going to make some phone calls then he's going to pick us up."

Without warning Lara's faced erupted in a flood of tears. She flung her arms round Emily's shoulders and wept freely into her friend's neck. The crowd watched in awkward silence.

Slowly Lara's sobs subsided. She took an offered handkerchief from Harry and blew noisily into it, growing quietly more embarrassed now she was recovering from her public outburst.

The crowd had broken, like a pool of spilled water, into little puddles of quiet conversation. Some were at the road edge, looking up and down the street for a sign of the vet's station wagon.

Fifteen minutes later he still had not appeared. Jamie was fishing in his pockets for more coins to call the surgery again when Ellen shrilled, "Here he comes!"

The Volvo cruised to a halt and the five crowded in, leaving the throng on the pavement.

In response to their inquiring faces Harry called, "We'll let you know later." The car sped away.

Jeff's face was set and serious. Finally he said, "No need to look so glum. I've found them."

Lara closed her eyes, whispering a little prayer of thanks.

"You're the best," grinned Emily.

"Don't speak too soon," he said. He paused. "Kids, it was the Weasel who stole the goats."

"We know," said Jamie. They told Jeff about the vandalized shed, and Sunday and the weir.

Jeff continued, "How he found out where you lived I don't know; but he has. It was him that sent the slaughterhouse round for Nanny and Sunday. I rang them all. I was only just in time when I found the right one."

There was silence for a while, and Jeff said suddenly, "I think you ought to give them up. Let me find them a really nice home somewhere, out in the country. Where the Weasel won't ever find them."

Even with his gaze fixed on the road ahead he could feel their eyes on him and the horror on their faces.

"Give them up!" gasped Lara, aghast.

"You could visit them," he added lamely. "An animal like that should be out in the country anyway, not hemmed in by a big city."

"What's wrong with the way we look after them?" said Ellen indignantly.

"Nothing. Nothing at all. Truly. I don't think anyone could have done better. But this man, this Weasel . . .I think he's mad; nuts; off his tree.

"To tell you the truth, I'm terrified of what he might do next. To the goats . . .even to you. Something really terrible . . ."

They were still pondering his words when the car slowed.

The station wagon turned in through a pair of high, heavy metal gates. A man in wellington boots and a vast rubber apron that reached to his ankles was hosing down the yard. The car hissed through the water as it drove in.

Another man appeared carrying a long, heavy knife. A brief, unheard conversation passed between him and the man with the hose. Both laughed loudly before the man with the knife walked away, through a sliding door into the building behind them.

The car slowed to a halt. Jeff applied the brake and turned to the children. "Will you think about it at least, please . . .?"

They nodded, not really listening. Their eyes were fixed on the yard and the man with the hose.

"Look at his apron," whispered Harry.

The apron was slick with water from the hose and streaked with a deep red, almost black. "That's blood," said Harry.

The others stared in silence. A spasm of shivering passed through Lara. Jeff stepped from the car and the rest of them joined him. The man in the apron saw them, recognized Jeff and raised an arm in greeting. He threw the hose down and walked over. He was big and beaming, but the children found themselves retreating from his vast, blood-stained apron. He didn't seem to notice.

"Hi, Mr Anderson," he said with a smile. "Hi kids."

They didn't answer. Jeff returned the greeting.

The man knew what they had come for.

"Wait here," he said. "I'll go and fetch the little blighters."

Lara shivered. "I hate this place," she muttered.

A huge door in the metal wall of the building slid aside with a rumble. It revealed the man in the apron holding Nanny on the end of a piece of twine passed through her collar. Sunday was pressed into her side.

Lara's face broke into a wide beam. "Nanny!" she cried, running forward.

The others ran with her as the man stepped out to meet them. At the sound of Lara's voice Nanny began tugging at the twine.

As they ran across the yard they were able to see deeper in through the vast doorway that had been slid open. A rail snaked back and forth across the ceiling, and from it hung an endless row of hooks, and from every hook there hung a carcase.

They were pigs. Their white skin was waxen and their ears hung limp, covering their dead eyes. The rows of hooks were snaking slowly on rails which looped across the building towards an interior door. The door was open and clouds of white vapour billowed through it, devouring the pale carcases as each one passed through. The dead pigs were being moved into the freezer room.

Men in rubber aprons were sluicing down the bloody floor with hoses. Another man carried a metal tray filled with an array of knives and cleavers.

Nanny nuzzled into Lara and the other children crowded around Sunday; but their reunion was overshadowed by the march of the hanging bodies through the slaughterhouse. The children couldn't take their eyes off them.

The man in the apron followed their gaze. He laughed loudly. "Want to take a closer look, kids?" he roared.

The children flinched. Lara looked up at Jeff. "Can we go, please?"

He nodded. They walked the goats over to the station wagon and while Jeff made space for them in the rear the man went on. "Lucky you rang when you did. Another five minutes and, fsssst!"

He made a motion with his hand across his throat. "Still, no harm done, eh?"

He turned to the children. "I'm sorry, kids. We took 'em in good faith. Never realized what the score was until Mr Anderson rang. Better be more careful next time. Good luck."

They climbed into the car. Jeff thanked the man and with a wave of his hand they drove away.

For a long time no one said anything. Lara was the first to speak. "Can we have a look at it, too? If you find a home for them. To make sure it's all right?"

There was a clamour of disagreement from the others. Lara waved them all to silence. "Don't you see?" she cried. "Another few minutes and that would have been Nanny. And Sunday. Hanging by their back feet!"

The others were silent, their thoughts returning to the slaughterhouse and the pigs and the men with their knives.

"Don't you see?" she repeated in quiet desperation. "Now the Weasel knows where they are he's not going to stop. He's mad. He won't stop until they're dead.

"You know how I feel about Nanny. I'd do anything rather than risk her being hurt. Even if I never saw her again."

Nobody said anything until the car had stopped outside their homes. Jeff switched off the engine and turned in his seat. "It would be for the best,' he said gently.

"Could we go and visit them sometimes?" asked Harry.

Jeff nodded. "I'll take you myself. I've got a place in mind. I'll have to ask them first, of course. They've got a herd of Anglo-Nubians. I'm sure they'll be delighted."

By the time they returned Nanny and Sunday to the shed, dusk was beginning to fall. Graffiti still stained the walls inside and out, but the bedding was clean and a fresh bunch of leaves hung from the roof.

The goats seemed unaffected by their ordeal. Jeff helped bed them down for the evening. He had bought a padlock which he secured to the door as they left. Nanny was quietly chewing the cud, curled on the bed of hay with Sunday beside her.

Lara turned to Jeff. "When do you think you'll know?" she asked quietly.

"I can ring them tonight. If it's okay we can take them tomorrow. It's well out of town. The Weasel will never know."

"Not too early tomorrow. We'd like to make a bit of a fuss of them before they go."

"After lunch? You can all come with me. They've got dozens of goats. You'll love it."

They all nodded. Wearily they followed Jeff back to his car and waved him goodbye.

It was gone midnight before the streetlights went out, leaving the houses as just a thicker shade of night in the moonless air. At the far end of the road a pair of headlights rounded the bend. The chugging engine cut out and the battered truck cruised silently to a halt.

The lights went out, fading quickly to nothing in the darkness. They were replaced by a thin torch beam within the cab. A figure climbed out carrying the torch, leaving the cab door ajar, a rustling bundle in its other hand. The figure headed for the side gate to the gardens. Once there it threaded its way along the narrow tracks, guided by the torchbeam.

Finally the figure stopped and the torchbeam rose and shone upon the word *Gippos* sprayed in red. The figure crept across the open space and stopped at the shed window. The torchlight shone through the spray-paint, lighting the interior with a faint red glow. Nanny raised her head and bleated softly. The sound drifted gently out through the open fanlight window.

The torch snapped off and the figure put it down. It reached up, raising the rustling bundle to the narrow fanlight. With a grunt of effort it shoved until the bundle fell through, hanging by a long cord which the figure tied to the fanlight catch.

Nanny eased herself from her bed and trod lightly over to the hanging bundle. She nosed at it gently. Her tongue snaked out and coiled round a dry leaf, tugging it free and retracting with it into her mouth. As she chewed, her tongue came out for another.

Outside the shed the clearing was already empty. The silent figure was hurrying back along the lane and into the truck. It spluttered into life and pulled away from the kerb. One rear light shone with extra brightness as the truck braked at the corner and, rounding it, disappeared from sight.

Eight

Lara woke in the half-light of dawn and lay listening to the chorus of birds in the garden. She had slept only fitfully through the night.

Her disturbed dreams had all been about Nanny. The slaughterhouse man with his bloody apron was chasing them – her and Nanny – among the butchered carcases of the pigs. He had a cleaver in his hand. Lara slipped and she and Nanny fell on the hosed floor. She tried to rise but she couldn't . . . and she could hear the steps running closer and the raucous laugh of the slaughterhouse man.

But the steps changed to a whispering scurry and the laugh became a thin whine; and when she looked up it was the Weasel standing over her paralysed body.

When she finally woke her thoughts were still of Nanny and the sad recollection that this was the last day they would be together in the garden.

She knew Nanny belonged as much to the others as to her, but that didn't stop her feeling a personal, exclusive love. She felt that somehow by immersing her whole soul into caring for the sick Nanny she had breathed her own life into the creature; that it had in some way become a part of her; not only Nanny, but Sunday, too.

The dawn chorus had stopped. The soft, early morning light acquired sharp edges, picked out on her bedroom wall in the sun and shadow, mottled here and there by swaying branches outside her window.

She looked at her clock radio. She had an hour in which to milk, muck out the shed and change the water before the others were up.

It would be a quiet time of her own that she would be able to treasure. There would be lots of kids from outside later, too. After the previous day's excitement they would all want to know what had happened. They were unanimously devoted to Nanny and the kittenish, clowning antics of Sunday. There would be other tears besides her own, she thought, when they learned the goats were going away for good.

Her feet, in trainers, were soaked in dew by the time she reached the shed. The garish graffiti was harsh in the morning light. She found the padlock key under its stone at the back of the shed, undid the lock and eased the door carefully open. Nanny and Sunday had a habit of standing eagerly on the other side. On more than one occasion they had received bruised noses as the door was flung aside.

This time there was no one the other side of the door to greet her. An acrid smell wormed its way past her nose. Threaded through the bitterness another smell, cloying and thick, also hung in the air. She heard a plaintive bleat. Lara could see Sunday, white coat turned to pink in the light from the red, paint-stained window.

The young goat was nosing into the still form of Nanny, who lay on the floor beside her.

At first Lara stepped forward gingerly, bewildered by the strangeness of her reception: the red-stained Sunday, Nanny still lying on the floor, the smells she couldn't place; unfamiliar, yet somehow remembered . . .

Then it came to her: it was the smell she had met in the Weasel's foul shed; the sickly-sweet smell of dying.

With a gasp she flung the door wide open and ran forward to Nanny, throwing herself down beside the still form. She recoiled from the vomit which lay in a stinking green pool around Nanny. More of it was spread over the floor.

Nanny's muzzle was coated in green mucous and her sweat-soaked flank pumped harshly. Her breath crackled in her throat, a strained and desperately rapid gasp for life.

Lara's face was a mask of stunned disbelief, her thoughts drowning in panic. One hand went to her horrified, open mouth while the other gently and briefly caressed Nanny's long silky ear. The goat's eye swivelled where she lay, and a tremor ran through her sweat-flecked body.

Next instant Lara was up and through the door, screaming out for the others as she ran. "Jamie, Emily . . .!"

Tears were already coursing down her pale cheeks as she burst panting through her back door. Her stricken cries had woken her mother who had flung on a dressing gown and stood listening with alarm at the foot of the stairs.

She watched as Lara snatched up the telephone book and desperately flung the pages aside in her search for Jeff's number. Her whole body shook and she was muttering distractedly to herself, "Please make it all right. Make it not true. Please make it—"

Her mother, eyes aghast, grabbed Lara by the shoulders, "What is it? What's going on?"

Lara shook herself free and punched out the number she had found. Only when it had connected and she was waiting for Jeff to answer did she turn to her mother and sob, "Something awful's happened to Nanny. She's not moving. Get the others."

There was something about Lara's desperate tone that prompted her mother to do as she said. By the time she had gathered the others – already woken in any event by Lara's stricken cries in the garden – the telephone had woken Jeff. They listened behind her as she blurted out the story to him through her body-shaking sobs. Their faces paled in silence.

Lara hung up and turned her red-shot eyes to the others. "He's coming straight away. He says to keep her warm – and to keep Sunday away from her. She's not to suck any milk."

Her gaunt, tear-stained eyes filled them with dread. She barged past them and fled back to the shed. They were close behind. Their parents, bewildered by the early morning confusion, were not long in following.

At the shed nothing had changed. Once again Lara flung herself down beside Nanny. Behind her a gasp of stunned horror rose from the other children and their parents. The questions in their minds were choked to silence by the sight of Nanny's tortured body, stretched full-length, and the bewildered Sunday, bleating softly beside her. Lara lifted the mucous-coated head into her lap, shaking her head and rocking silently over the distressed and panting body.

Sunday poked her nose into Lara's ear, nibbled at her hair, and turned to nudge at Nanny's udder. Through her grief Lara remembered Jeff's instructions. She turned to the others. "We've got to keep Sunday away from her. Jeff said."

Jamie nodded and together he and Emily gently led the bleating kid aside.

Lara turned to Ellen. "Can you find something warm to cover her with," she whispered.

And to Harry, "Maybe we could clean her up a bit; if you could get some warm water . . ."

Harry nodded. Before he or Ellen could move, Lara's mother was already removing her dressing gown. "Use this to cover her. Go on, don't worry. I'll go and get a coat. I'll get some warm water and some towels while I'm at it," she said gently.

Nanny's breathing had grown less desperate. Her lungs ceased their urgent pumping and the movement in her flank was barely discernible.

Lara never left her side. The others took turns to nurse the fretting Sunday. Every face wore red-rimmed eyes and a grim dread of what might lie ahead.

They covered the shivering Nanny and had cleaned up most of the vomit, gently bathing Nanny's muzzle, by the time Jeff arrived.

He came running along a track from the side gate, veterinary case in his hand. He ducked into the crowded shed and in one glance took in the solemn faces and the prostrate form of Nanny. His own features became set with concern.

His manner grew businesslike. "Let's have some space in here. I need more light and a bit of room to work."

Both parents and children began to shuffle out with Sunday among them.

Ellen looked up solemnly and said, "She's going to be all right, isn't she?"

Jeff forced a smile. "Just give me a little while," he said, non-commitally.

As they left the shed he eased a hand under Lara's elbow. "You'd best leave it to me," he said gently. "I'd better not waste any time."

Lara's mouth collapsed as she looked up. "What can it be, Jeff? She's got to be all right. Please? Make her better . . .?" More tears coursed down her cheeks.

He placed his hand on Lara's hair and whispered, "You know I'll do everything I possibly can, don't you? I promise."

She nodded miserably as he gently lifted her from the floor and guided her to the door. "Just check with the others if she's eaten anything unusual, and take care of Sunday. She'll be frightened by all this."

He closed the door of the shed and turned back to the still form of Nanny.

Outside, Lara's mother gently placed an arm round her daughter's shoulders. The other parents formed a solemn group. Emily was crouched with an arm over Sunday's shoulders, caressing the kid's flank. Harry stood with his back to everyone, hiding his distress, his hands wringing a leaf into shreds. Ellen was holding her mother's hand, her face serious and her tongue silenced.

Jamie stood a little distance away, close to the front of the shed, kicking miserably at a stone. As he stood looking down he noticed two marks in the turf: pronounced indentations where the toes of a pair of boots had dug deeply down. They were beneath the window.

His eyes rose to the shed wall. He saw through the graffiti a deep graze scored into the ancient, mossy planks by a metal toe-cap.

"Look at this," he called, his eyes lifting further.

As the others followed his gaze he said, "Someone's been here. These marks are fresh. Someone's been trying to get in this window or something."

He reached up and found the string attached

to the fanlight catch. He drew it out. There were still a few leaves caught in the loop at its far end. "What are these? We don't have anything like this in the garden, do we?"

Emily's father took them from him. "They're rhododendron leaves. It's a big flowering shrub. They might be in here somewhere. They used to be keen on rhododendrons in this kind of garden."

Lara was peering at the leaves. She shook her head firmly. "No. Nothing like that. I'd have noticed because I would have wanted to know if they were safe for Nanny to eat."

Emily's father hesitated. "Well . . . I hope not. I believe they are poisonous – to cattle anyway."

"How did they get here, then?" asked Jamie and Ellen's mother.

Jamie looked across at Lara. "I think we can guess . . ."

Lara shuddered. She put her hand to the painted window and tried to peer through. "I wish he'd hurry up," she whispered.

As if in answer to her thoughts the door swung open. Jeff stepped into the sunlight, his face care-worn and tired. In his hand he carried some leaves like those Jamie had found.

Lara crossed quickly to him, her eyes wide and questioning. He placed a hand gently on her shoulder and held up the leaves.

He said wearily, "I heard you from inside. You're right. They are rhododendron leaves; and they are poisonous to goats, even more than to cattle, probably. Nanny must've eaten them. The symptoms are classic. She must have eaten quite a lot. Too many . . ."

Something in his tone turned Lara's stomach to ice. She felt the chill crawl over her body. Even as she ducked past Jeff his arm was restraining her.

He crouched beside her, his gentle hands squeezing the tops of her arms tight. "Lara," he whispered. "I'm sorry. I'm so sorry. There was nothing I could do. She'd eaten too much of it."

He watched as Lara's eyes widened with horror and her mouth tried silently to form words that wouldn't come, and her whole face began to collapse and crumple like a broken dream.

His own eyes filmed with tears as he said softly, "She's dead, Lara. I wish it wasn't so, believe me. But she's dead."

He never moved as Lara twisted herself free. Blind with tears, her face contorted in an agony of grief, she ran to the shed.

Nanny lay just as she had a few minutes before, the red light of the window paint staining her body. This time there was no movement, not even the faint rise and fall of the breathing flank; there was no sound, not the faintest tremor of breath in her throat.

Lara flung herself down on the body and the pain of her distress rent the air, cleaving through the walls of the shed, echoing round the clearing and driving like a nail into the hearts of the others where they stood.

Emily flung herself into her mother's arms,

smothering her sobs against her breast, while Ellen, lifted up by her mother, wailed deeply into her neck. Harry buried his head on his arms against the side of the shed. His father, himself consumed with grief, comforted him awkwardly. The other adults sniffed back tears and turned away from one another and still the sound of Lara's misery cut through the sunlight, chilling them all.

To one side Jamie was crouched beside Sunday, his arms round the kid's neck, his own head buried in its shoulder. His back pumped with violent sobs as his tears flowed into the kid's coat, soaking through the white hair and running to its tiny cloven hooves.

For many minutes the group stayed like this, their own choking misery acting as a background to Lara's keening. Gradually this diminished until the only sounds were the soft punctuation of sniffed-back tears against the chirruping of birds in the trees around them.

A soft bleat from Sunday broke the spell. Jeff lifted himself wearily to his feet and stepped into the shed. One by one the others followed.

Lara was spread over Nanny's back, her head pressed against the coat, her eyes staring blankly at the wall, unblinking. Jeff placed a hand on her head.

"There's still Sunday," he said, directing the words not only to Lara but to the others as well. "You remember when you said Nanny stayed alive so she could have Sunday?

"Well, they need you more than ever now. Both

of them. You have to take over Nanny's job for her. Sunday's got to be fed . . ."

He paused, but there was no response. "I – I'm sorry . . .I let you down. After everything you did . . ."

For the first time Lara stirred. She lifted her swollen eyes from Nanny's back. Her face was expressionless and when she spoke her voice was a monotone. "That's not true. No one could have known it would come to this."

She looked to each of the others. "Jeff's right. It's too late for Nanny. But whatever happens we have to keep Sunday safe, for Nanny's sake."

She turned back to the still form of Nanny, and gently rubbed her nose along one silky, drooping ear. She studied the head, the long throat and the flanks, her eyes travelling the length of the goat's slender legs. Finally she put her lips to the soft Roman nose and kissed it, before climbing unsteadily to her feet and trudging out of the shed.

Nine

They dug Nanny's grave at the edge of the clearing where the evening sun danced on it through the overhanging trees. The parents helped, and they wrapped Nanny's body in a blanket and lowered it down. They spaded the earth in over her until a mound of moist, fresh dirt marked the spot.

Children from the streets around watched in mournful silence while Emily and Lara marked the smooth mound with rows of flints. Harry nailed two lengths of wood together to make a cross with the one word, Nanny, painted across it. Sunday, confused and uncomprehending, trotted from one to another with a constant, soulful bleating.

As Jeff had said, Sunday needed them more than ever now. He provided them with milk powder which they mixed with warm water to feed the kid. It wasn't easy to educate the tiny creature to suck at their fingers, which they then lowered into the bucket of milk; but in this way, gradually, the kid would learn to drink for itself.

It was still agreed that, for her own safety, Sunday would leave the following day, as soon as Jeff had time to make the arrangements.

Lara and Harry's parents were happy to allow the kid to spend the night in the house. It was unthinkable that Sunday should be left alone in

the shed after the horror that had been brought to her there.

The visitors wandered away, leaving Jamie and Harry, Lara and Emily each with their own grim, unhappy thoughts. Ellen, too young to fully understand their grief, was full of questions: "But how long does it take to *get* to Heaven? Why can you only go there when you're dead?

How's she going to get there now we've buried her?"

Eventually her mother, understanding that the others did not appreciate the child's ceaseless chatter, dragged her in for an early bedtime.

The remaining four stayed a little longer, needing the companionship, but not knowing how to form their thoughts into words, since words were inadequate. Although it was never said, they were all worried about Lara.

Since her first abandoned outburst she had withdrawn inside herself. Her body seemed drained not only of tears, but of flesh and colour, and even spirit. She had said nothing since the few words she had spoken to Jeff.

It was Jamie who first said what was on all their minds.

As they prepared to split up for the evening he said quietly: "It wasn't your fault, you know. No one could have known what we were dealing with."

Emily added, "He's right, Lara. We'd already agreed to let Nanny go. It was just one day too late."

Lara snorted grimly. "One day! I reckon we were a lot later than that. Months too late.

"You know what I think? I think that in some strange way poor Nanny was always doomed; that she was only ever holding out long enough for someone to rescue Sunday.

"Well, we did. And I think that's the good that must come out of all this – Sunday."

She looked around to the others for confirmation, her dull eyes suddenly burning with an angry light. "Right?"

They nodded.

"Whatever happens we must take care of Sunday," she said fiercely. "If anything happens to her then we'll all be to blame. If anything happens to her then we were wrong and we should have let Jeff end their lives right at the beginning."

The others studied her in awkward silence, not knowing how to respond to her savageness. Finally Jamie said, "I think we all understand that."

Lara pushed the door open. "Goodnight," she called and disappeared into the house.

Later, when her parents had gone to bed and the house was in darkness, Lara slipped out of bed and padded downstairs to the kitchen where Sunday lay curled on a rug.

"Shh," she whispered as the kid embarked on a soft, welcoming bleat. She coaxed Sunday to her feet and led her upstairs to the bedroom. Sunday leapt on to her bed and settled there for the night. Lara lay awake a long time, thinking back to her times with Nanny, her tears soaking the pillow.

The following morning they had to face the grim memories of the shed. They cleaned out the old bedding and washed down the floor while Sunday walked between them all, nosing curiously into their faces, bleating constantly. They mixed the milk powder and fed it to her, but still the kid fretted and wailed for Nanny.

No one spoke much. They all feared any words might choke to tears in their throats. Instead they tried to play with Sunday, tried to make the most of their last hours with her before Jeff arrived to take her to a new home; but their hearts weren't in it. Even Feather was content to lie in the shadows, his head resting mournfully along his legs.

Lara sat on her haunches by Nanny's grave, a grass stem between her teeth, her thoughts fenced away from the others behind her bitter eyes.

Jeff arrived shortly before midday, sombre and unsmiling like the children.

"Well, it's all organized," he sighed. "It's the same people who were going to take both of them. When I told them what had happened they were really upset. They said you were welcome any time to visit.

"They've got dozens of goats and some of them are, well . . ."

His voice, which had been growing more enthusiastic as he spoke, grew suddenly quieter, "just like Nanny, really . . . And we could go over together maybe, at weekends . . ."

He could see the spark of interest grow in every eye except Lara's.

He studied her until she returned his gaze. "What d'you say?" he asked.

She returned the warmth in his eyes and even allowed a faint smile to cross her mouth before she said, "We couldn't have done any of it without you. We didn't have a clue at first, just lots of enthusiasm. Well, if we let our enthusiasm run away with us, it'll be Sunday who suffers."

She looked to the others. "How would we ever know we weren't followed? What if the Weasel found out through us where Sunday was and did the same thing to her? And maybe the other goats?"

She shook her head. "No; I hadn't realized before, but we have to say goodbye to Sunday here and it has to be for good. The Weasel's taken them both away from us, just as completely as if they'd both died."

The others opened their mouths to argue, but before any words came another voice interrupted them. The sound of it grated over them like barbed wire over concrete.

"Truer than you think," it wheezed, the last of the words dying away into a snigger. "Damn kids."

At the edge of the clearing stood the Weasel, the glint of triumph in his eyes. There were two other men with him.

The colour drained from the friends' faces. They sidled closer to Jeff. Emily clutched Sunday, drawing her away from the Weasel. Behind them they heard Feather's growl rise like distant thunder.

For a brief moment Jeff's mouth hung open in surprise as he saw the Weasel; then it snapped shut, setting itself in a thin, hard line. His eyes

117

narrowed. They could sense the rustling in his body, like smouldering paper in the moments before it bursts into flames.

He opened his mouth to speak, but the Weasel beat him to it.

"Don't waste yer breath," he snarled.

He pointed to the men with him. One was dressed very like the Weasel and was the same height, though thicker in the body. He was grinning, but there was no humour in it. The other wore a dark suit and carried a brown envelope in his hand.

"This is me brother," growled the Weasel, indicating the first man.

Thumbing towards the second he added, "An' he's from the courts."

He squinted at the five friends, showing his two rodent-like front teeth, and said to the second man, "Tell 'em what we've come for."

The man in the suit stepped forward. He cleared his throat, holding up the envelope. "I am an officer of the Crown Court and I have here an injunction authorizing me to take custody of one goat kid, the subject of a hearing to be held in the Crown Court on Friday next to establish ownership of the animal in question."

He handed the envelope to Jeff who snatched it from him and tore it open. As he studied it the man added, "I'm sorry about this, sir. I don't like it any more than you do."

The Weasel scowled. "Save yer sympathy. I'm after my rights. It's the law and it's on my side."

118

He stepped forward, his arm outstretched for the kid. He was brought to an abrupt halt as Jeff's arm stabbed out, holding the Weasel back with ramrod fingers against his chest.

The Weasel shrugged uneasily, his tongue running over his lips as he waited for Jeff to finish reading.

Jamie edged forward and stole a look at the letter. "But he's banned from keeping goats. This is a trick. It has to be." He turned to the man in the suit. "Why would a judge let him take Sunday back? He's been banned for five years." Jamie's voice began to rise. "He's even poisoned one . . . !"

The Weasel turned to the man in the suit. "You listenin'? That's slander.' He turned back to Jamie. "Unless you got any proof a-course," he scoffed.

Jeff interrupted him, his voice grim and grey. "It's not him that's after Sunday." He tipped his head towards the third man. "It's his brother."

The others all looked at Jeff, uncomprehending. He went on, "He's claiming that before he was banned he had already sold Nanny to his brother. Therefore, as the kid was Nanny's, it's now legally his brother's."

Emily's voice burst in, "But we got her at the Weasel's place, *after* he'd been ban—"

Suddenly she realized what she was saying and her own hand came up and clamped over her mouth.

The Weasel's accusing finger was stabbing

119

directly at her as he turned to the man in the suit. "I want you to witness that. I told you they stole 'er."

He turned back to Emily, his ragged teeth exposed in a broad, ugly grin. "I only had 'er there temporary. She escaped from me brother and found her way back. He was comin' over for her when you lot nicked her."

"You liar!" screamed Emily. Jeff's hand restrained her.

He turned to the man from the court. "Is there any way we can challenge this?"

The man shook his head. "The court felt there was sufficient grounds for believing the kid might disappear unless the injunction was granted. That's why I'm to take custody of it. Now."

He saw the horror in the children's eyes and added, "But that doesn't mean anyone else will get their hands on her. She stays with me until the court decides who is the legal owner."

Lara had joined Emily and Sunday at the back of the group. "What if we won't give her up?" she asked.

The Weasel interrupted. "Then you'd be breaking the law," he scoffed. "An' you so keen on courts, too. Well, they're on my side now. Gimme that goat."

Lara's eyes held a deep, cold hatred. Whatever ability to frighten her the Weasel might once have had, he frightened her no longer.

She observed him levelly, barely concealing her

120

contempt. "What do you want with Sunday?" she asked.

The Weasel's face blazed into purple rage. "I'm going to have her skin! And it'll hang on my wall to remind me of you!"

His eyes gleamed with a wild light as they bore into each one of the group in turn. "Interfering brats!"

He regained control of himself and added shiftily, "Leastways, it's me brother who owns it now. It's down to 'im." His mouth twisted into a cruel grin, matched by his brother standing just behind him. The children shuddered.

"I ain't got time for this," growled the Weasel. "Gimme the goat and let's get out of 'ere."

Lara ignored him. She turned to the man from the court. "How are you going to look after Sunday? Since her mother was killed . . . poisoned," her eyes burned through the Weasel, " . . .she needs hand-feeding, with milk powder. Can you do that?"

The man shook his head. "Not me personally, miss. I'd put her into the hands of a professional person, pending the court hearing. A vet, something like that."

There was silence for a second, as the words sank in. Then Jeff gasped, "I'm a vet. Why can't I keep her in my care until the hearing?"

The Weasel scowled. The man from the court hesitated. "Well . . .if you have a vested interest it might not be—"

"I'm their vet," proclaimed Jeff innocently, spreading his hands wide. "I'm only here by chance this morning to check the kid over. If you come out to my car I can show you my credentials. My sole concern is the welfare of this animal."

Once again the man in the suit hesitated. "I'd need your professional word . . ."

"Naturally," said Jeff grandly. "I fully understand my responsibility to the court. The goat will be cared for until the hearing when she will be delivered up pending the judge's final decision."

The man smiled. "Very well. I find that most satisfactory."

Emily gripped Jamie's arm in excitement and Harry and Ellen, who had been watching in silent horror, hugged each other with delight, hardly able to conceal their grins.

Only the Weasel and his brother were dissatisfied. "It's a set-up," snarled the Weasel. "I'm takin' that goat; and I'm taking it now."

As he moved forward the man snapped, "I warn you that if you do you will be guilty of contempt of court. That's a serious offence."

They all watched as the Weasel's mouth twisted into a cruel knot of angry frustration. "I can wait," he spat.

He stabbed a forefinger threateningly at Jeff. "Just make sure you're there, with that." He indicated Sunday, "Or you might find a few of your patients start gettin' incurable diseases."

Jeff's face was a mask of disgust, but he said nothing. The Weasel turned on his heel, his brother at his shoulder, and stamped away, still limping slightly from the wound in his foot.

The court officer heaved a sigh of relief and turned to Jeff. "Unpleasant business," he said. "Now if I could just accompany you to your car and establish a few things – where the goat will be kept and so on . . ."

Jeff turned to the others. "I'd better take Sunday with me. I won't be a minute."

He scooped the kid into his arms and led the court officer out of the garden.

He returned with Sunday when the court officer had left, to find the five children in an excited cluster. They mobbed him enthusiastically, their faces split with broad grins.

"Well done," said Emily. "You were brilliant."

Harry said, "Now all we've got to do is get her out of here. How far away is the farm?"

Jeff's brow furrowed. "What do you mean?"

"Well, she's got to be well away before the court case. Somewhere the Weasel couldn't even begin to find her."

"I don't think you understand," said Jeff. "Sunday will be at that court when she's wanted. I gave my word."

Their mouths dropped open one by one. Only Lara seemed unsurprised, her cool eyes studying Jeff.

Ellen spoke first. "You must be barmy. This might be our last chance to save her!"

"I understand how you feel, but don't you see . . .I promised," implored Jeff. "If I hadn't offered, Sunday would already be gone. He'd have taken her now. Somewhere you couldn't find her at all."

"But what if the Weasel wins, Jeff?" muttered Jamie. "She'll be as good as dead."

Jeff swept his fingers through his hair, and flung his hand down against his thigh with a frustrated slap. "I don't know. We'll have to get

a lawyer to represent us. I'll find a good one; I've got a few contacts."

He raised his hands, imploring: "Look, I'm sorry. Please understand, I can't break my word. We'll win somehow . . ."

Lara spoke for the first time. "Jeff's right. He's a vet. He can't break his word. He has to be there. So does Sunday. And us. All of us. We'll get the whole neighbourhood. They'll see who's right and who's wrong."

She gave Jeff a fond smile and he returned it; but behind the gentle light in his eyes his thoughts were saying: "But life's not like that. Sometimes the people who are right are the ones who suffer."

Ten

By the day of the court hearing there wasn't a boy or a girl within half a mile who hadn't heard about the threat that was hanging over Sunday.

The five friends had found it hard to say good-bye to the kid as she walked away with Jeff, but they knew she was in good hands. He treated her like a pet dog. She travelled with him in the car, and rather than leave her overnight in the lonely, clinical, veterinary pens at his surgery he took her home with him. She tried to eat the curtains and kept him awake at night with a continual lonely bleating.

They saw her regularly, and would have missed her more if their minds had not been filled with plans to swing the court case in their favour.

They had travelled with Jeff to see a lawyer who beamed when he spoke to them, but when Emily asked him outright, "Well, will we win – or won't we?" all he would say was, "It's not that simple."

"We can't rely on *him*," said Lara, shrugging him off as an irrelevancy. "We've got to do something ourselves."

They travelled the neighbourhood, talking to group after group, plotting a campaign to save Sunday.

When the day of the hearing arrived, in street after street, everyone left as usual for school. Along with their schoolbags, under almost every arm was a rolled bundle.

On ordinary mornings they trudged to school in desultory groups, spinning out the conversation, putting off the moment when they passed through the school gates and into lessons.

But this morning was different. Individuals joined to form small groups, and the groups joined to make gangs, and the gangs turned into a throng of children, stepping purposefully forward with Lara and Jamie, Harry, Emily and Ellen at their head.

They marched up to the school gates and past them, and on into the city centre and the large, imposing stone building that formed the county court.

The rolled bundles were unfurled and a forest of banners waved above their heads:

SOS – Save Our Sunday.

The Weasel's a Killer

End Cruelty Now

The words, thickly written in coloured paints across a maze of plundered bedsheets, gave a carnival atmosphere like flags at a fair; but the cries of the children were strident and angry.

"We want Sunday. S-U-N-D-A-Y, Sundaaay!" they chanted.

A lone policeman scratched his head, and talked urgently into his pocket radio.

In the midst of the chaos a car, sleek and big and black, driven by a chauffeur, carefully threaded its way through the crowds. In the rear sat Mr Justice Carmichael, the judge who would decide Sunday's fate. He studied the crowds and the banners and sighed inwardly.

Once inside the courthouse he changed into the official wig and gown in which he presided over the cases brought before him. As he did so the clerk of the court outlined the morning's work. The chant of the crowds outside drifted in through the windows.

"How in God's name, Mr Wicks, are we supposed to do any work this morning with that racket continuing? Can't they be shifted?" asked the judge.

"I understand they're here for a case, your honour," replied Mr Wicks, nervously. He had an unsettling feeling that his well-ordered court might not run according to plan.

He outlined the background to the affair. He had already heard from members of his staff – who had heard it from their own children, who heard it from children who went to school with Lara and her friends – about the rescue of Nanny and her subsequent death. The Weasel's cruelty case in the magistrate's court was already common knowledge among the court officials.

The judge listened with interest. As the story unfolded, a small, reluctant smile crossed his face and his eyebrows raised in evident surprise. He crossed to the window and eased a gap in the blind so that he could see the crowds of children, their banners swaying, their voices calling in unison, "S-U-N-D-A-Y, Sundaaaay!"

As he watched the chant changed to a cheer. A car drew into the court car park: a green station wagon. It purred to a halt and out of it stepped Jeff, not in his veterinary clothes, but smartly dressed in a suit. With him was another man, a lawyer carrying a sheaf of papers, who was to represent the children in court.

Jeff walked to the back of the station wagon and threw open the tailgate. Sunday stood for a moment on the rear platform of the car, her plaintive bleat lost in a roar of delight from the children. She skipped lightly down, held by Jeff on the collar and lead that had once been Nanny's.

There was a light of admiration in the eyes of Mr Justice Carmichael, but he kept it to himself. Judges were expected to be impartial. It would not do to let Mr Wicks think he favoured one side or the other.

He dropped the blind and turned back to the clerk. "Well, Mr Wicks, this promises to liven up an otherwise dull morning, don't you think?"

Mr Wicks nodded, groaning inwardly.

"We'd better take this case first," the judge continued. "We won't be able to hear ourselves think until we do."

He strode for the door. "And pack as many of those young people as you can into the public seats. We don't often get a chance to show them how their legal system works; might as well make the most of it."

Mr Wicks shook his head in silent exasperation. If he'd had his way he would have kept as many as possible *out*. Crowds meant trouble; goodness knows what a crowd of children might do.

The courtroom was humming like a power station generator. The court officials had done as instructed. The public seats were jammed with children. More stood shoulder to shoulder at the back of the courtroom.

The courtroom door was pushed slightly ajar and a vertical row of heads peered in through the crack, passing details in whispers back to those packed in the corridor, who could not see. From the corridor they spilled into the open, down the steps into the courtyard.

On the far side of the car park, a lone figure leaned idly against the Weasel's battered truck. Sean had seen the throng, and decided it might be safer to hear the court's verdict later, rather than among the hostile crowd.

The children were overwhelmed by the solemnity of the courtroom. A huge royal crest looked down from behind the high seat in which Mr Justice Carmichael would soon take his place. A hubbub of muted, murmuring voices filled the room.

The angry eyes of the children drilled into the backs of the Weasel and his brother, sitting at the front of the court with another man, their lawyer. The three of them sat facing the judge's bench, their backs to the public seats.

Occasionally they exchanged whispered comments and scowled across at Jeff and the five friends, also sitting at the front but on the far side, well away from the Weasel. Huddled down among their feet was Sunday, trying to hide herself from the commotion.

A uniformed court official opened a door to one side of the judge's bench and the room dropped suddenly into silence. His voice boomed, "Please rise for his honour, Mr Justice Carmichael."

The judge swept in through the door and strode to his seat. His gown billowed like a sheet on a line. In his white judge's wig he looked older and sterner. The whole room shuffled obediently to its feet; even Sunday, who was panicked by the sudden sounds of feet and scraping chairs. Jeff held tightly to the lead while Emily soothed the frightened kid.

The judge looked up suddenly and his eyes bored into the crowded public seats. When he spoke his voice was clear and penetrating, brooking no argument. "Good morning. I'm delighted to see so many of you taking an interest in the proceedings of the court. However, before we begin there are some important matters which must be made clear.

"This case will proceed in the normal manner and there will be no – I repeat, no – interruptions from the public seats. If there are any such interruptions then I shall have the court cleared. I hope this is understood because I shall not repeat it. You may listen, but you may not speak unless you are called as a witness."

Without hesitation he dropped his eyes to the two groups at the front of the court. "Now, who appears for the plaintiffs?"

And so the case continued. First the Weasel's lawyer outlined his client's case, then the Weasel gave evidence, followed by his brother. Both were cross-examined by the children's lawyer.

There were gasps of horror from the public seats as the Weasel's brother told the court, without so much as blinking, that he was fond of goats and was looking forward to giving Sunday a good home. Mr Justice Carmichael hammered loudly with his gavel and sharply demanded silence, which he got.

At first, when the judge issued his warning to the court, Lara's heart sank to her feet. But as the case progressed it became clear that, much as he might try to hide it, the judge didn't like the Weasel nor his brother. He sighed irritably at their replies, snapped at their lawyer for his slowness.

132

By contrast when the children gave evidence he was patient and pleasant, helping them to form their thoughts, urging them to take their time. Gradually the details came out of Nanny's rescue and the subsequent birth of Sunday.

Even when the judge reprimanded their lawyer for bringing a goat into court, he did so lightly, with a smile in his voice.

"As the poor creature is directly relevant to the case I shall let it pass," he said. "But don't make a habit of it."

Lara's hopes began to rise. She leaned into Jeff and whispered, "I think he likes us."

The lawyers summed up their cases. The children had begun to fidget in their seats as both men went on at length, quoting precedence of past cases, reiterating important points that had come out in the proceedings.

Finally the judge announced that he would adjourn briefly while he considered his decision. The official's voice boomed out, "Please rise!"

By the time everyone had shuffled once again to their feet the judge had swept out of the room.

The pent-up excitement in the crowd burst out in a furious chatter of opinion. "He was on our side . . . no, he wasn't . . . he could see what the Weasel was like . . . he wouldn't let them win, would he? . . .wish he'd hurry up."

Lara and the others heard it all as they sat in silence at the front of the court, not daring to discuss it with one another. Lara had taken Jeff's hand and through it he could feel her trembling with anticipation. Her eyes stared into the middle distance and her mouth was set in a grim line.

The other four were buried in Sunday's coat, stroking the kid, soaking up every inch of her as if it was their last chance.

Jamie turned to the lawyer who was sitting with them and murmured, "What happens if he wins?"

"I'm afraid he takes Sunday," he said gently.

"What, now? Straight away?"

The lawyer nodded. Jamie turned silently away, a sudden grey doubt pouring like a cold mist into his stomach.

Time ticked by. Gradually the excitement diminished and was replaced by an expectant, impatient hush. The uniformed official appeared once more and cried. "Please rise."

As they did so Mr Justice Carmichael swept back to his seat.

He beckoned forward the children's lawyer. "Bring those children with you, and Mr Anderson," he ordered.

They lined up in front of the judge's bench. Jeff still held Sunday on her collar and lead. They could see the judge's weary eyes, and the creases in his brow as he looked down at them.

He paused, surveying each of them in turn. Lara sensed he did not know how to begin and it frightened her.

"I've listened very carefully to everything that has been said," he began.

"And I think it is important you should know that you have my greatest admiration for your efforts. You have shown resourcefulness, responsibility, care for the suffering of animals. I imagine Mr Anderson . . ." he looked across at Jeff, " . . .and your parents are very proud of you.

"However . . ."

The word sliced into Lara's mind like a blade. "However . . .however . . ."

She felt her knees tremble and her own thoughts reply, "Oh no, oh no!"

The judge's voice went on, " . . .the issue here is one of ownership; and there has been no evidence to suggest that the case put for the plaintiff is not a matter of fact. They claim that ownership of the dead goat, Nanny, had already passed to the brother.

"How Nanny came to be in the shed where you found her is perhaps a matter which should be taken up by the police, but my job is to administer the law in this case . . ."

The words were coming to Lara as if through a tunnel. They were a whispering echo in the distance as her own thoughts raced, seeking for a door out of the impossible madness that was drowning her in words.

" . . .And therefore I have no alternative, under the law, but to declare that Sunday's rightful owner is the man here, and that she should be returned to him forthwith."

With a tired sigh the judge indicated the Weasel's brother. Both men had already risen from their chairs, triumphant leers splitting their faces.

"However," snapped the judge, turning hard

eyes on the two men. "I shall also instruct the appropriate authorities, as a part of my decision, to ensure that no unnecessary suffering is caused to this creature."

Lara heard the words and understood with a hidden dread what they meant: a quick death at the hands of a slaughterhouse butcher was not considered unnecessary suffering; she knew that. Sunday was still to die.

Jeff's arm curled round her shoulders. For a moment she wanted to bury her head into his side and burst into tears, but she knew it was senseless, hopeless. Her eyes blurred, she shook her head to clear them and Sunday fell into focus, shaking her own head on the end of the collar and lead, unaware that her life – no, her death – had been decided.

The Weasel and his brother were pacing across the room to collect their trophy . . . their revenge. An idea blossomed in Lara's mind. A foolish idea, but it was too late to care now. Anything . . .

She reached up to Jeff and whispered in his ear. Jeff listened and nodded. He looked up to the judge.

"Your honour," he said. "Lara has asked if she might have Sunday's collar and lead. While the court has decided that Sunday does not belong to her – nor indeed to any of us – ownership of the collar and lead has never been questioned. I can confirm that the children bought them and they have a great sentimental importance, belonging first to Nanny, Sunday's unfortunate mother."

The judge studied Jeff, turning over the words in his mind. "I can see no harm in that," he said. "Your reasoning is sound."

He smiled sadly at Lara, grateful for the chance to help them salvage some small consolation from their loss. "You may keep the collar and lead."

Lara smiled shyly back. She sensed the irritable muttering from the Weasel and his brother a few steps away. The Weasel was stripping a grimy leather belt from his trousers, to use in place of the collar and lead that Jeff was removing.

Lara watched as Jeff carefully freed the buckle. The collar fell from Sunday's neck.

Lara took a step back. With all the strength she could gather in her sturdy body she flung herself at Jeff. He was bent over, unsuspecting, and the force of her charge felled him like a tree.

"Run, Sunday!" screamed Lara. "Run, run!"

The kid went rigid, for a moment petrified with shock. The crowd behind, stunned into silence by the judge's decision, suddenly woke up to the words Lara screamed. A great roar of approval swept through the room like a storm.

For a moment Jamie, Emily, Harry, Ellen, the lawyer, the judge and Mr Wicks all stared in open-mouthed disbelief; then they recovered. A clamour of voices urged Sunday to run while Mr Justice Carmichael hammered impotently with his gavel. "Order! Order! Clear the court! Clear the—"

It was too much for Sunday. With a blare of alarm she suddenly sprang on all four feet to a nearby desk. From there she leapt again, to the

137

judge's bench. For a brief moment they faced each other nose-to-nose, the judge paralysed with surprise, before Sunday was off.

She bounded round the room in terror as the cacophony swept over her. She cannoned into an usher and sent him sprawling. She leapt the low rail that divided the public seats from the body of the court and sped down a narrow corridor

which opened through the crowd of children as she ran.

The Weasel and his brother, faces contorted with rage, chased after her. They got no further than the rail before Jamie's well-placed foot brought the Weasel down. His brother stumbled over him, tripped and fell, and the crowds of children closed around them.

The courtroom door swung wide and Sunday fled through, tail up, fear lending her speed. She raced through the thronging, roaring children. The only gap she could see led down the corridor and out through the open door into the sunlight.

Mr Justice Carmichael was on his feet. "Stop that animal!" he cried. "Stop those children! Order! Order!"

Two burly policemen appeared and were struggling through the masses, trying to make sense of the chaos. They had no idea which children the judge meant.

The Weasel and his brother were striking out at the confusion of children around them. The brother was up first while the Weasel, one hand holding up his trousers, searched through the milling feet for his belt.

Sean had drifted off in a reverie of his own when the roar from the courthouse interrupted his thoughts. The noise crashed through the open doors like a wave. He watched as the sea of children parted. From the gap a small white creature burst like a bullet.

Sunday tore across the car park, into the road and out of sight. A car horn sounded and Sean watched as the vehicle lurched to the far side of the road, its tyres screaming in a painful slide. It stopped with a crash of glass and metal. Across the street Sean watched a lamp-post topple. More car horns rent the air; someone screamed and Sean caught a brief glimpse of Sunday as she disappeared down a side road.

Back at the courthouse Jeff and the five friends appeared through the main doors. They stood breathlessly at the top of the steps. Lara looked nervously up at Jeff. "I couldn't let him take her," she mumbled. "I'm sorry."

Jeff nursed a bruised rib where he had cannoned into a desk as he fell. He smiled at her grimly. "We'll worry about that later. We've got to find Sunday. She's in as much danger out here as she was in there with the Weasel."

A boy at the foot of the steps pointed, "She went across the street, that way."

"We've got to find her," called Jeff to the crowd. "Spread out, three or four together. If you find her don't run after her. She'll be terrified. Send someone back to tell us. Quickly!"

A cheer went up. The crowd spilled across the car park like water from a bucket. Jeff turned to the five friends. "You'd better go, too. You've got a better chance of finding her than anyone else. She'll come for you. And in any case – things aren't going to be too healthy for you here. Hurry. I'll try to explain to the judge."

He waved them away. They ran as a group across the car park and out of sight, unaware that Sean was watching them from behind the Weasel's truck.

Jeff hurried along the corridor back to the court, pushing his way through a few straggling children still chattering excitedly. Suddenly the Weasel and his brother burst through the courtroom doors, hurling children aside as they went. The Weasel's eyes were narrowed, his jaw set with a poisonous, deadly fury.

He fixed Jeff with his glare and stabbed him in the chest with a finger. His voice was thin and hard with rage. "Always you! Everything I do, somewhere you turn up to get in my way. Well, I won't forget you! When I've finished with you you'll wish you'd never crossed me. Better not turn your back for too long."

He hurried away, his fists clenching and un-clenching with frustrated rage.

Outside, he strode across to the truck. Sean saw the blind anger that reddened his bloodshot eyes.

"I–I saw the goat," Sean blurted, pointing. "It ran across there."

The Weasel's hand shot out and caught the boy a stinging blow across the side of the head.

"And you let it go!" he shrieked. "I paid you good money to help me."

He snatched hold of Sean's jacket lapels, dragged his face within an inch of his own, baring his two yellowed, weasel teeth. "You snivelling brat! Find it; or I'll take it out on you instead. I'll have the truck waitin'. On the next block, by the cinema; there's a Chinese restaurant. I'll be in the alley beside it," he growled.

"And don't try and run off home, see. Or I'll come lookin'."

He flung the boy aside, slamming him against the high side of the truck. Sean gasped as the breath was punched out of his body. He edged his way past the Weasel and ran out of the car park.

141

Eleven

Lara, Emily and Harry split up. Jamie was slowed down by Ellen but still, with the help of their friends, they scoured the network of streets around the courts.

They asked passers-by if they had seen a goat. They called in at shops, stopped cyclists, waited at traffic lights and knocked on the car windows always with the same question: "Have you seen a goat, a young one, white with one black ear?"

And always the answer was the same: a blank look and a shake of the head.

Now and then they could hear children in other streets calling, "Sundaaaay!" But there was never any cry of delight to follow as a sign she had been found.

The morning passed into afternoon. It had been more than an hour since Lara heard any other person calling for Sunday. Her own voice echoed back at her as she explored a backstreet far from the city centre where the old terraced houses were being torn down to make way for offices. The boarded-up houses offered no clues.

She walked on past an empty plot where some of the houses had already been demolished. The wind swept across it, picking up the dust, sweet wrappers, bits of plastic, and throwing them down among the docks and nettles.

Nettles.

Lara felt her skin prickle. How could she have been so stupid! She wondered how many patches of nettles she must have passed as she trudged from street to street. Sunday loved nettles. Back in the garden they were the first thing she learned to eat. She curled up to sleep in them like a fawn in bracken.

She forced her weary feet into a trot, trying to remember where else she might have passed a patch of city weeds.

She criss-crossed her way back towards the city centre, checking the forgotten corners of dusty parks and playgrounds, where the council mower had been unable to reach in and cut down the undergrowth. She checked side alleys and empty blocks; and when she was more than halfway back to the courthouse, in a patch of bindweed and nettles hidden behind an advertising hoarding, she found Sunday.

The kid was curled in a corner, its head tucked forlornly under the warm fold of its hind leg. Lara almost missed her as she stood among the tall weeds and softly called Sunday's name. No reply.

She made to turn away, back to the road, and through the breeze-blown greenery she glimpsed a little spot of incongruous white. It was Sunday.

She pressed the warm and trembling body into her own, unaware of the nettle stings she had received as she ran through the weeds. Tears of relief dripped into the kid's coat.

For long minutes she lay with Sunday, the sounds of city traffic deadened by the hoarding and the thick weeds. She searched her mind for a once-and-for-all answer.

She couldn't take Sunday back to the courthouse to be handed over to the Weasel.

She would take the kid out of the city by the back streets. With luck she might make it; she *must* make it. Somehow she would find a farm that would take Sunday in. She had some money for a bus fare, and if that didn't take her far enough, well – they'd walk it.

She unthreaded the long laces from her trainers, tied them together to make a lead and knotted one end round Sunday's neck so it wouldn't slip. She coaxed the nervous goat up from its nest and set out down a side road, away from the bustle and noise, heading for the quiet areas where Sunday would relax a little more and they would be less likely to meet other searchers.

They rounded the first corner and almost fell over Sean as he slouched against the wall.

Lara was frozen with horror like a mouse trapped by a snake; then she turned and ran, dragging Sunday after her.

It was hopeless. Sean would have caught her easily enough without Sunday to hold her back. He grabbed Lara's arm, almost lazily, and yanked her to a halt. She flung herself round on him like a caged animal, snarling her rage. Her fists flailed at his chest and she screamed, "He's going to kill her! Don't you care? You stupid fool! Can't you do something that's right for once! Just once—"

There was a sharp crack as Sean's open hand swung into her cheek. She stopped, and only then took notice of the boy who stood before her.

His eyes were red-rimmed, as if he'd been crying, and his cheek-bone bore a heavy graze. There was no vindictive pleasure in his face, as she had seen before. He looked grim and frightened. He had one hand on the lead just below the point where it wound around her palm.

"Shut it," he snapped. "I ain't done nothing wrong. I was only helping the Weasel get his property back. I ain't gonna suffer just because you can't keep your thievin' hands to yerself."

Lara was bewildered. "Why should you suffer?" she asked.

"You don't know 'im. He's crazy. He's freaked out. This thing . . " he indicated Sunday " . . .goes back and then I'm out of it. I don't wanna know no more."

The tears began to flow down Lara's cheeks. "Please don't do this."

"I'll give you anything; we all will. Please Sean." As Lara spoke she tried to prise his hand off the lead.

145

He set his jaw and with both hands yanked hard on the thin shoelace. The cord bit deep into the soft outside edge of her palm, burning its way through the skin. Lara screamed with pain. She threw herself at Sean, her arms swinging wildly, desperately, at his head. A grunt of effort accompanied every blow.

Sean grabbed blindly at her, his fingers reaching into her dark hair. He swung her with all his force first one way then the other, throwing her off balance. He dragged her in a half-circle and flung her like a rag doll into the gutter. She skidded over the tarmac; her head jerked back and cracked into the sharp edge of the kerbstone.

She lay stunned. She could see the blurred figures of Sean and Sunday walking away. Drunkenly she staggered to her feet and stumbled after them. "Please don't," she wept. "Please don't."

As she recovered she made more desperate attempts to stop him, but her senses reeled from the blow to her head and she was no match for his strength.

She yelled for the others, for Jamie and for Jeff, but there was no answer. She tried coaxing Sunday to stop, but the kid could not. Sean ignored her presence behind him; just kept walking, dragging Sunday with him.

All Lara could do was follow, impotent to interfere, hoping that somewhere in these empty side roads full of parked cars and quiet houses she might meet someone who could help.

She grew puzzled. She had expected Sean to head for the courts, but instead he was skirting widely round them. She followed a few yards behind, her head clearing all the time, waiting for Sean to make a slip – but he never did.

It wasn't until he turned into the alley beside the cinema that she realized it was all too late. A truck filled the narrow lane, facing them. The Weasel was sitting at the steering wheel. There was no sign of his brother. She saw the cruel grin spread over the Weasel's face as Sean and Sunday stepped into view.

"No!" she screamed. "No, you can't!"

She leaped forward, dragging her weight against the lead in Sean's hand. Sunday bleated mournfully. Once again Sean locked his fingers in Lara's hair and flung her into the wall at the alley entrance. Her back pounded with a hollow echo into the bricks and she lay winded, tears choking in her chest.

She heard the truck cough into life and watched as the Weasel shoved open the passenger door. It banged against the wall in the narrow alley. Sean lifted in the struggling Sunday, and at the command of the Weasel squeezed in himself.

The door slammed, the Weasel crunched the truck into gear, and it lurched forward. Lara flung herself around the corner of the alley to avoid being crushed. The truck wheezed out, across the pavement to the road, pausing momentarily for a gap in the traffic.

Lara snatched the chance. She jumped painfully

147

to her feet and flung herself at the rear of the truck. As it drew away she hauled herself in among the grease and the junk that clanked and bounced around her.

Lara lay low and still in case the Weasel should see her in his rearview mirrors. The flat bed of the truck rattled and banged against its ancient, withered springs. Lara's teeth rattled in her head. A heavy lump of iron jolted and bounced, trapping her fingers. She bit back the pain and wrenched them free.

She began to think: there were now two of them. She had been powerless against Sean; what could she do against the Weasel, too?

And where were they heading? She crawled on her stomach through the oily litter to the truck's side. She peered cautiously over. They were in the city centre one-way system, busy with traffic. The truck turned to one side and a signboard went past. They were on the road to the court!

Lara slumped brokenly to the bottom of the truck. So all her effort would be in vain, after all. Sunday would be returned, officially, to the Weasel's brother. She would not be given a second chance to cheat them. Her face crumpled. Stained with oil and grime and tears, she peered over the edge of the truck. It hardly mattered whether the Weasel saw her now.

She could see the courthouse car park, and over the cars she made out the figure of Jeff, with Jamie beside him. Jamie was talking to someone who was hidden by the parked cars. She guessed the others had given up their fruitless search and returned to the court.

But the truck wasn't slowing. She felt the Weasel move into a higher gear; the truck gained speed. Lara's heart lurched. Her thoughts were in chaos. If he wasn't stopping maybe there was a chance, but not on her own.

Whatever the Weasel was planning she needed help. Her only chance of getting it was there, in the car park.

She had to let them know. Somehow . . . maybe if she yelled. But among all the traffic they wouldn't hear it. There were cars and motorbikes, buses and lorries behind and in front.

Her eyes fell on a ragged, rusting section of car body beside her: a rear wing, clattering in the filth of the truck bed. She lay on her back and put her feet against it, shoving with all her strength. At first it wouldn't move, then it jerked free on the oily waste and slid towards the open end of the truck. In the car behind the driver watched in disbelief. He sounded his horn cautiously, just a brief hoot.

Lara ignored him and shoved once more. The jagged metal slid over the edge, hit the ground with a tortured, rending groan and clattered and bounced into the road behind the truck.

The car behind shrieked to a halt on screaming tyres, while the driver kept his hand down on the angry horn and screamed abuse.

"I think somethin' must've fallen off the back," cried Sean in alarm.

"Tough. I'm not stoppin'. Not here. Not by the court. Damn fool judge. Damn the law," snarled the Weasel. "I'll do it my way, now."

The clatter of metal, the scream of tyres and the angry horn made the crowd in the car park look up. They saw the car lurch as it braked, but the truck ahead of it meant nothing to them. Only Harry and Ellen had seen it before, when the Weasel was waiting near the pedestrian crossing, but they hadn't realized to whom it belonged.

They turned away, more concerned with their own loss and misery. All except Ellen. She saw the small, dark head peering over the truck side, and the arm that waved.

"It's Lara!' she screamed.

The sudden, shrill alarm sent a tremor of shock through them all. They spun round to where she was pointing. They saw the truck for a brief second longer before it drove beyond the open area and was hidden by buildings.

"That truck!" screamed Ellen. "She was in the back of that truck!"

The others looked doubtful. "Are you sure?" asked Jamie. "I know what you're like."

"It was, it was!" Ellen was hysterical with frustration. "She must've pushed something off to warn us! We've got to follow it." She tore at Jeff's hand, dragging him towards his car.

"Funny," said Harry, "but I'm sure I've seen that truck somewhere before."

Jeff gazed to where a line of traffic had piled up behind the stopped car. Someone was lifting the torn metal out of the road and tossing it on to the pavement.

He made up his mind, lifting Ellen from the ground as he did so. "Well we're not doing any good here," he cried. "Come on!"

He ran to the station wagon, the others on his heels. By the time he had flung Ellen into a seat the others were already in and slamming the doors. He flung himself into the driving seat and turned the ignition. The car squealed into a tight reverse turn, braked and shot forward. It cleared the car park entrance ahead of the traffic which had been stopped by Lara's jettisoned wreckage.

There was nothing between them and the truck but time, but there was no sign of the battered vehicle in the street ahead. They sped on.

From the rear seats Emily called, "How do we know it hasn't turned off?"

"We don't," yelled Jamie from the front passenger seat as he peered intently at the road ahead. "We just have to hope – STOP!"

The sudden yell made Jeff leap in his seat. He rammed his foot down hard on the brake. The car slewed as it slithered to a halt.

Jamie poked his thumb back the way they had come. "Back there, by that side turning. There's a pile of junk lying in the road."

Jeff rammed the station wagon into reverse and it whined back to the missing turning. At the corner lay some oil-soaked cardboard.

Lara only took her eyes off the road behind long

enough to find something in the truck she could throw to mark their route. It was all she could think of.

It had to be something soft, paper or rags, or the Weasel would hear it and grow suspicious. But as Lara scanned the road behind, her hope began to flag. She had seen Jeff and the others look up at the noise of the braking car and the crash of metal, but she hadn't been able to tell whether they spotted her waving.

And even if they did follow, she realized with despair, there was very little chance they would spot *every* sign she had thrown in the road. They only had to miss one to be hopelessly lost.

And she was running out of material. She was coated in a filth of black oil. It streaked her face, smothered her arms and soaked into her jeans and sweatshirt. Still she dug in the grime for more missiles. Soon all that would be left would be the heavy lumps of junk iron that rattled and banged around her.

She looked over the truck side and was surprised to see she knew exactly where they were. They were in her home territory; she recognized every road. The truck lurched into another corner and Lara shoved another lump of oil-soaked cardboard off the back. They had turned into Riverdale.

She had friends here. If only they would pass one; she could shout a message . . .

But the streets were empty. The truck banged on, down hill. They passed the entrance to her own road and Lara punched at the truck bed

152

with frustration to think how close they were to home.

Lara grew still as she wondered why the Weasel had come back here, back to her territory, where the risks must be greater. She knew he must have a motive; the thought nagged at her like dark clouds on an ominous horizon.

The cloying smell of oil reached down and filled her stomach. Nausea rose in her throat and burned at her tongue. The truck made another turn and Lara shoved the last load into the road behind them. They were heading for the river.

Fear gripped her as she heard, above the clatter of the truck, the distant roar of the weir.

Twelve

The truck grumbled to a halt on an area of wasteland about a hundred metres upstream from the weir. Lara knew the spot. The land had been occupied by a rowing club, but the buildings had been removed years ago. All that remained was a slipway, from which skiffs had once been launched, and an ancient wooden jetty, its planks mouldy and rotten, to which bigger craft had once been moored.

Lara pressed herself down in the truck, sick with dread, the stench of oil rising in her face. She heard the truck doors slam and the scrunch of gravel as Sean and the Weasel walked away, towards the river.

"What are you going to do?" she heard Sean ask nervously.

She peered over the edge of the truck. The Weasel had Sunday's thin, shoelace lead in one hand. Sunday was dragging along on the end of it.

In the other hand he carried a sack. It was of brown and coarsely woven hessian, and it was big. Lara shook her head, not believing what she saw.

"No," she mouthed, "Please, no." But no words came.

On trembling legs she dragged herself to the edge of the truck and lowered herself down. She stumbled across the gravel, watching as the Weasel held open the sack with one hand. With the other he forced Sunday's resisting head into the opening. Lara heard the panic in the kid's voice as it pealed out a note of uncomprehending fear.

She ran forward, her horror giving her new strength. "Stop it," she screamed. "Let her go, let her go!"

She yelled to Sean as she ran. "Are you going to let him? How can you! Do something!"

But Sean stood petrified, not daring to interfere.

The sack was closed. Only the thin cord of the lead was visible, snaking out where the Weasel held the neck squeezed shut in his fist. The brown bundle convulsed in his hand as Sunday panicked in the dark, smothering interior.

With a couple of twists the Weasel had tied the neck shut with the protruding lace. He stood, gripping the sack with two hands, and lifted it high over his head.

As he turned to the jetty's edge Lara leaped. Her hands locked on the hessian sack, her extra weight dragged it down behind the Weasel. He

155

cursed violently, swinging a fist at her. She hung on like a terrier, mute and desperate.

Sean watched, horrified, as the Weasel, his eyes small and wild with rage, dragged the sack to the jetty edge. Still Lara hung stubbornly to the coarse cloth.

The Weasel drew back his lips and spat, "You, too, then, damn you!"

He lifted the sack once more, this time dragging the weight of Lara with him. Sean started forward, "No," he cried. "You can't. She'll go over the weir. She'll drown."

The Weasel paused, turned towards this unexpected interruption. Sean looked into the red, raging eyes and quailed.

"Keep out of this," snarled the Weasel.

Sean tugged at Lara, "You've got to come away," he yelled. "He's crazy."

"Help me first, help me with Sunday," she wept.

"I can't, he'll—" Something else grabbed the boy's attention. He pointed. "Look!"

The green station wagon was speeding down the hill towards them. They watched as it leaped the kerb, careering and bouncing across the waste ground towards the truck.

The Weasel saw it, too. He gave a howl of fury and gathered his strength to fling the sack. Sean grabbed his arm. The Weasel tried to shake him off but the boy wouldn't have it.

"The girl will go, too," he cried. "You can't!"

The Weasel dropped the sack. If Lara hadn't

156

been holding it Sunday would have bounced over the edge of the jetty into the swirling current below. She dragged the sack from the edge while the Weasel, lips drawn back in a vicious line, struck Sean a heavy blow on the chin.

He hit him again and again and the boy stumbled back off the jetty under the barrage. His knees sagged and he collapsed heavily to the concrete, lying still where he fell.

The Weasel stood his ground, his eyes filled with malice as he scowled down at the unconscious boy. Lara was struggling with the sack, trying to untie the tight knot at the neck. Before the Weasel could turn back to her he heard the sound of car doors slamming. Jeff, Jamie and the others were out and running across the gravel.

A strange sensation caught at the Weasel's thoughts. Something out of place grabbed his attention. For a second he felt . . . off balance, as if the earth had slipped beneath him. Then he felt it again, more violently. He looked down and saw the planks beneath his feet open with a groan, and close again. Behind him Lara cried out in fear.

The ancient jetty, tired and mouldering, had given up. The rusty bolts and the sagging supports could take no more. There was a sudden lurch and the Weasel was thrown down.

The other children froze with horror. Only Jeff was still running forward. He yelled, "Run Lara! Leave the sack. Get off! It's going to collapse!"

She dragged herself to her feet as the Weasel did

the same. She gripped the sack with both hands, the small body still struggling inside, and began to drag it across the swaying platform.

"Leave it!" screamed Jeff as he ran. "Or you'll both go!"

The jetty began to tilt. There was a sound of ripping timber as the last of the ancient pilings parted from their rusted bolts and the whole structure swayed drunkenly. It paused a moment, then slid like a sinking ship into the river. They watched in horror as the cold, brown water closed over Lara's head.

As the jetty collapsed the Weasel leapt for solid ground. One foot hit the water. He hooked his fingers into a ridge in the concrete and dragged himself to safety beside the unconscious figure of Sean.

Lara surfaced among the torn timbers as they swirled and buffeted around her in the current. Water coughed and choked from her nose and mouth and eyes. She was still clutching the sack.

Jeff stood at the bank, his eyes wide, his hands clutching at his temples. "Oh my God!" he cried.

Already the current was dancing around Lara, sucking her faster and further out. She struggled to keep a grip on the sack as it thrashed wildly in her hands.

Jeff turned. "The weir bridge," he yelled. "It's the only chance."

He sprinted away. The others tore after him.

The Weasel, bent and breathless, watched with a wild gleam in his eye as the floundering figure

158

of Lara was teased by eddying whirlpools out into the turbulent river.

He heard the drum of feet on the wooden boards of the weir bridge. Jeff, followed by Jamie, Emily and Harry, and Ellen a long way behind, raced on to it to cut off Lara as she passed beneath.

The Weasel's eyes narrowed. He snorted angrily, muttering a string of invective as he watched.

Jeff leaned over the single rail of the bridge. A fine mist hung around him as the breeze blew spray up from the weir torrent.

"Watch your step," he bellowed to the others above the roar. "It's slippery."

Jamie joined him. Already Lara was surging forward as the current picked itself up for the plunge into the cauldron of the weir pool.

"We'll never reach her!" yelled Jamie. "It's too far down."

Jeff threw himself on to the planks and stretched. He was more than a metre from the surface of the racing flood. He pulled himself up. "A stick or something, quick!"

"There's no time," cried Jamie.

Lara was struggling to keep the sack above water. As it thrashed in her hands her own head vanished beneath the surface. She came up gasping and choking only a few metres from the bridge. The current had her in its grasp, sweeping her relentlessly forward.

Jamie threw himself on to the planked bridge, his back towards Lara. He held one of the rail uprights for support.

"Grap my legs," he yelled to Jeff, "Maybe I can swing down trapeze-style."

"You'll never hold her, the current's too strong!"

"What choice do we have?" shouted Emily, who had run up with the others. She pinned one of Jamie's legs to the boards.

Jeff joined her, and then Harry. Jamie released his hold on the post and threw his body backwards into the void.

The river was a dark, menacing hiss in his ears as it swept past a few centimetres below his outstretched fingers. For a moment panic seized him. There was no sign of Lara. Then her head appeared once more. She was still straining to hold the sack clear of the water.

An eddy sucked at her and she was spun round, twisting off to one side. To his horror Jamie realized she had been pushed away from her track directly beneath him. He was going to miss her!

Her head rose gasping out of the torrent. Jamie swung his body violently to one side, straining every ligament to give him extra reach. He clutched blindly with his fingers.

He felt something sweep them, absurdly gently, like seaweed in a summer pool. He closed his hands and his fingers locked on to Lara's hair. He gritted his teeth and hung on as the thundering water tried to suck her out of his grasp. He feared it might tear her away, ripping the hair from her head. Then he felt her hand clutch at his wrist.

He brought his other hand over and grabbed

Lara's wrist. Slowly the weight of her body sank back against the current. Jamie released her hair and grabbed her wrist with both hands, while she retched the brown water of the river from her lungs.

Jamie heard Jeff scream, "Let go of the sack. For God's sake, Lara, you must! It's the only way."

Jamie said nothing. All the strength at his command was concentrated on his aching fingers; but he saw Lara's eyes open as she heard Jeff's voice. He saw the firm shake of her head through her exhaustion.

Jamie's fingers were stiffening with effort and Lara's wrist, slick with river water, began to slip. He yelled up, "Harry, climb down. Try to grab the sack. I can't hold her much longer!"

Harry watched the force of the river bite at his sister's clothes and he quaked inwardly. He heard Jeff yell over the thunder of the weir, "Don't be a fool. It's too risky. Let go of the damned sack!"

Harry looked at his sister's pale, bedraggled face as the current tore at it. All the risks they'd taken, all the pain they'd suffered; he knew she would never let go. She would be dragged with the sack into the boiling, torrent of the weir, but she would never let go.

He dropped to his knees, grabbed hold of the rail support, and began the slow descent, finding toe holds in Jamie's clothes, clinging desperately to his legs.

Jeff was wild-eyed with fear. "Get back!" he screamed. "You'll all go. It isn't worth it."

But he dared not move away from Jamie's legs. He turned to Emily. "I can hold him. Go and stop Harry."

"But—"

"Go!"

Emily crawled to the side of the bridge. Harry was already half way down. He had a hand in Jamie's belt and was trying to reach out for the sack. He was too far up. He switched hands in the belt and tried again. Lara tried to heave the sack up a few centimetres more. Harry threw all his weight against Jamie's belt and his fingers closed on the hessian.

The struggling within the sack had grown feeble, but still the weight of water made it impossible to lift. The realization drained the colour from Harry's face. He looked up at Emily, an edge of panic creeping into his voice. "I–I can't lift it. It's too heavy."

Lara still had one hand on the sack. Now that the burden was shared she found some small reserve of strength. Beating up through the water with her legs she shoved the sack higher still. Harry used the extra height to strengthen his grip, drawing himself up as he did so. The sack was clear of the river.

As water drained from it he drew in his arm, grunting with the effort. Lara released her hold and Harry strained to lift the bundle level with his chest. Emily lay flat, stretching down to help.

162

Below them Jamie grabbed for Lara's hands until he had a firm hold on both wrists.

Harry felt with his foot for a more secure toe hold. He searched out Jamie's jeans pocket and lodged his foot there, heaving himself up. Emily's fingers had barely closed on the sack when the pocket ripped away, and Harry slid down with a terrified yell. He hung grimly to the belt, clawing his way up, feet scrabbling against Jamie's body for purchase. Emily struggled to retain her hold on the sack.

"Ellen," she yelled. "Help me."

The small girl flung herself on to her stomach and reached down. Her tiny fingers plucked at the hessian. They had no strength to lift, but they gave Emily a brief second in which to adjust her hold, to gain a secure grip with both hands.

She wrenched the sack higher. As it came, Ellen, too, was able to grab a firm hold. The sack inched its way up until it was over the edge. It lay in a wet pool on the bridge.

"Undo it and get Sunday out," shouted Emily above the roar of the weir. "I've got to help Harry."

A hundred metres away by the collapsed jetty the Weasel watched with mounting disbelief. He foamed with blind fury as the sodden bundle was dragged on to the bridge. He uttered strained notes of impossible rage in his throat as Emily caught hold of Harry's hands and helped him to safety. Lara inched her way up Jamie's extended body towards the outstretched hands above and the Weasel's cheeks were veined with purple.

He whirled round, back to the truck, threw open a door and scrabbled behind the back seat. When he drew his hand out again he was gripping the handle of a heavy billhook, its curved blade gleaming dully under the film of oil which coated its razor edge. He strode off towards the bridge.

Finally Lara was high enough for Harry to reach, then Emily; even Jamie could push from below. Lara was dragged on to the wet boards like a landed fish. She lay exhausted on the narrow platform, shivering with cold and fatigue, river water rattling in her lungs. The others dragged Jamie up until he could reach the rail post and haul himself up by it.

Jeff's face finally crumpled under the strain. He choked back tears, sobbing to himself, "Crazy kids! My God, you crazy kids."

All this time Ellen's small hands struggled with the water-soaked knots binding the neck of the sack. Finally they surrendered to her worrying fingers and the neck fell open. Inside she could see Sunday's white, sodden hair. It was quite still.

She bit her lip and laid her hand on the chilled goat. She felt a tremor run through it and heard a gurgling sneeze. The shape in the sack scrabbled for a purchase, wriggling itself round until one black ear and a white Roman nose, wet and forlorn, poked out into the air. Sunday looked around through slotted eyes and wailed mournfully.

"Hurray!" shrilled Ellen, and the others laughed where they lay, despite the cold and the exhaustion.

Jeff shook his head and muttered tearfully, joyfully, "Crazy kids."

He pulled himself to his feet and leaned over Lara. "Are you well enough to move? We ought to get off this bridge."

She smiled and nodded, reaching out to take his hand. He helped her to her feet and she grabbed at the rail for support. Jeff hauled Sunday clear of the sack and gathered her in his arms. He shoved the empty, sodden sack into Ellen's hands. The others also climbed wearily to their feet.

"Now let's go," said Jeff, "before our luck runs out."

They took a step forward, but a new sound came humming down the length of the bridge towards them, telegraphing a new footfall on the planks. Jamie looked up.

"I think it already has," he said, nodding towards the far end of the bridge.

The Weasel was moving towards them, barring their path off the narrow walkway. He brandished the billhook, and though they couldn't hear him over the roar of the weir, they could see him screaming and spitting as he advanced.

"Get behind me," said Jeff. "Let me handle this."

They moved obediently back.

Jeff turned to Jamie. "Here, take Sunday. Get off the bridge and get out of sight."

Jamie wrapped both arms round the kid and trod carefully back along the walkway.

The Weasel was striding forward, his eyes wild

and red, his face a purple rage. Jeff stood his ground, waiting, giving the others as much time as possible to clear the bridge.

The gap between the two men closed. Jeff could pick out the Weasel's ravings as they hung in the spray from the thundering weir pool . . .

"My goats . . .the law . . .teach you!"

He advanced, swinging the billhook savagely, until the two men were an arm's length apart. The Weasel thrust the billhook menacingly at Jeff's chest.

Jeff studied the other man's face. A muscle had begun to twitch in the Weasel's cheek; his body was shaking and his face and throat were a web of dark veins. The corners of his mouth were filled with spittle. His eyes were pinpoints of deadly light, merciless as a stoat in the night.

"The goat's mine," spat the foam-flecked mouth. "I'll 'ave its skin; and those kids, too."

Jeff never took his eyes off the billhook. "You're already in enough trouble," he said evenly. "Get off this bridge and let them alone. A boy beaten senseless, a girl nearly drowned. You're insane."

The fury of the attack never gave Jeff a chance. The billhook swept through the air again and again, slicing at his head and arms. Blow after blow rained down, cutting into his coat, biting into the back of his hand and letting the blood flow.

On the far bank Jamie and the others watched. Ellen screamed, "Run Jeff, run!"

But Jeff dared not run, dared not take his eyes of the oiled blade. He cursed under his breath that the others had not fled out of sight as he ordered. He turned his head to yell at them and missed, for one swift atom of time, the strike of the billhook.

As the blade drove down he raised his arm to protect his head. The weapon sank deep into the flesh of his upper arm. Even before the Weasel had yanked it free the blood was soaking through the coat sleeve, scattering like rain over the planks and into the river.

A gasp of horror rose from the five friends. Jamie thrust Sunday at the others. "Here, hold her. I've got to help Jeff."

He looked around for a weapon, anything that might help, but the bank was clear. He snatched the dripping sack from Ellen and started back across the bridge.

Jeff almost blacked out from the pain of the cut, but he knew that if he turned away, if he took his eyes off the blade for an instant, the Weasel would strike. The man's reason had gone; madness drove him on.

Jeff lurched back against the iron rail. The billhook swept down and as he jerked his head back the blade clanged into the metal.

His whole arm was dyed with blood. It ran in a stream from his fingers and his hand hung useless by his side. He clawed his way backwards but the Weasel advanced, sweeping and striking with the blade. Jeff felt a searing pain across his cheek as the hooked tip of the weapon sliced open a flap of skin.

A drumming noise reached his ears. It sounded

167

distant, reaching towards him from the back of his mind, and he thought, "This is it; I'm passing out. I've had it."

But the noise was Jamie, feet vibrating through the boards as he sprinted along the narrow walkway. He watched Jeff's body sag and curl on the planks as it shrank from the storm of blows, strength drained out of it with the flow of blood.

The Weasel paused to take a two-handed grip on the billhook. He swung the weapon high over his head, gathering all his savage strength for the strike.

Jamie was too far away. A sob of hopelessness choked out of his throat and with one last, desperate lunge he hurled the sack.

The Weasel saw it. He twisted his body as the billhook sliced down, turning his face away to dodge the sodden, heavy hessian.

He took the full force of it on the side of his head. It knocked him off balance and the billhook missed Jeff, clanging into the iron rail. The Weasel's feet skidded on the wet and mildewed boards. He snatched for a hold on the rail and missed, tried to recover and leaned too far.

His back arched out over the water. The outstretched arms lunged in the air for balance. The wild, mad eyes of the Weasel filled with terror as his hands, one still grasping the billhook, windmilled desperately above the iron-brown, thundering torrent. He teetered on the edge of the walkway, his eyes peering insanely into the raging spume of the weir pool.

The roar of the torrent was drowned by the Weasel's scream as he toppled over the edge. The

sound and the man were gone, swallowed up in the thundering, frenzied, fury of the water below.

Thirteen

Jeff looked a hundred times better than he had when the ambulancemen finally arrived and carried him off the bridge on a stretcher. His arm was still heavily bandaged, held against his chest by a sling. There was a dressing taped to his cheek where the billhook had sliced into the flesh, and his hands still carried plasters where they had been hacked as he tried to protect himself.

He was sitting solemnly with Ellen on his lap. Jamie and Harry, Emily and Lara sat on either side. They showed no signs of their ordeal at all.

For days after Lara had been a source of worry as she lay totally exhausted, a smile on her face and Sunday curled at the foot of her bed. Now she was herself again.

She looked across at Alf and he winked, but not one muscle of his face, nor of hers, lifted into a smile. Behind them was a sea of faces – school friends and parents among them – and every one wore the same serious expression as they sat in rows facing towards the high bench at which sat Mr Justice Carmichael.

His face, too, was unsmiling.

He looked down on the Weasel hunched in the dock. The last the five friends had seen of him was when he was fished half-dead from the river, in the slack water a short way downstream from the weir pool.

The judge eyed him stonily, his voice booming down across the courtroom. This time it was a different, higher court: the criminal court of Quarter Sessions.

" . . .indeed, had you been given the chance to wreak your terrible revenge on your innocent victims, you might now stand convicted of a far greater crime: that of murder," said the judge.

"No thanks to you that you have been found guilty here today only of the most grievous bodily harm against a man who had the courage to stand between you and your own evil, savage desires.

"Nor is that the full extent of your viciousness. A boy whom you threatened and bullied into your service was beaten senseless by you and is only now recovering from his wounds.

"It is clear the public must be protected from your uncontrollable rage before some other person falls victim to your wrath.

"I therefore sentence you to seven years imprisonment."

A murmur rose from the public gallery and echoed softly round the courtroom. A policeman gripped the Weasel by the arm and led the sullen figure out of the court to a waiting prison van.

Ellen jumped down from Jeff's lap and said firmly, "Serves him right!"

The judge's gavel cracked sharply, twice, against its wooden block. An usher's voice bellowed, "Silence in court."

Mr Justice Carmichael leaned forward across his bench and said sternly, "I understand there are a number of young people in court in the company of Mr Jeffrey Anderson. Please have the group brought here before me."

A look of stunned horror dropped the jaws of all five friends. They looked to Jeff for rescue, but he had none to give. No question this time of knocking him down and running for the door.

Jeff stood up. They moved with him into the main body of the court. They had to bend their necks to look up at the judge's wigged head.

He peered down for long seconds, studying them. In sharp tones he said, "The last time we met, as I recall, you five attempted to make a mockery of the law."

They stood trembling under the bite of his words.

"Without the law, civilized society ceases to exist and we become little more than animals. This, after your recent experience, I am sure you now know only too well."

His voice rapped, "It will not be tolerated! Do I make myself clear?"

No one answered. Jeff nudged Jamie, whose dry throat croaked. No words came out.

172

Ellen looked up at Jeff and whispered loud enough for the entire courtroom to hear, "What's all that s'posed to mean?"

"Never mind," murmured Jeff. "Just say 'Yes, your honour.'"

They all mumbled the words.

Mr Justice Carmichael looked doubtful. "Mmm. I hope so. If such a thing occurred again it would be treated with the utmost seriousness.

"We will let the matter rest there. For the moment there are other considerations."

He picked up some documents from his desk and once again froze the group with his penetrating stare.

"Lara?"

She raised her hand nervously.

"It would appear you are in many ways the ringleader in this affair, as well I remember!"

She paled under his gaze.

"However, my information is that you risked your own life in an heroic action of the highest order to save a helpless animal from a cruel and unnecessary death.

"In this attempt I understand you were assisted by . . ." he read from the papers in his hand . . . "Harry?"

Harry shuffled a step forward.

"Emily and Ellen?"

The two girls joined him.

The judge studied each of them, too. "I understand that without your assistance the outcome of this affair might have been a considerable tragedy.

173

"I am therefore empowered to present to the four of you these testimonials from the Royal Society for the Prevention of Cruelty to Animals in recognition of your endeavours."

They were dumbstruck, hardly hearing the words as he rapped them out, hardly seeing as he handed the rolled and ribboned testimonials to an usher, who in turn handed them to each one of the four.

Jeff and Jamie exchanged wide-eyed, delighted glances. In the public seats the crowd erupted into excited chatter.

"Silence in court!" boomed the usher.

Mr Justice Carmichael continued. "I understand there is another boy? Jamie?"

Jamie blushed from the tips of his ears down past the collar of his best shirt. He stepped nervously forward.

The judge eyed him closely. "You sir, risked your own life to save that of your friends. You had the courage to put your faith in those around you, so that they might enable you to pluck Lara from a horrifying death.

"Not content with that you went to the aid of Mr Anderson against an armed assailant when you yourself carried no other weapon than a . . . er, a wet sack?"

Jamie nodded. A glimmer of a smile traced its way across the judge's face. Jamie allowed himself to copy it.

"Clearly everyone of you played vital roles in this dangerous episode," said the judge. "But none more so than Jamie, without whom two lives, perhaps even more, would have been lost.

"It is therefore my privilege to hand to him the Royal Humane Society's Testimonial on Vellum for outstanding bravery."

Again he handed the usher a rolled document to be handed on to Jamie. This time nothing could stop the cheer that burst from the crowded seats, nor the applause that echoed its way round the sombre walls.

When it had subsided the judge looked at Jeff and added, "You, too, sir, are to be commended for your actions. I trust your health is improving?"

"Yes, thank you, your honour."

"Quite so. I'm sure these young people are well aware of the great value they have gained in your friendship, as indeed you have in theirs."

"Absolutely, your honour."

The judge observed them all for a moment, then added, "There is only one outstanding matter: that of the ownership of an Anglo Nubian goat kid called, I believe . . ." he referred to his papers, "Sunday?

"I am informed that no other person has come forward to claim ownership since the matter was last held to be in question. I therefore pass her into your joint custodies. I have not the slightest doubt that she is in the best possible hands.

"Usher . . ."

At these words the usher strode across the room to a side door and pulled it open. Sunday, collar and lead restored, bounced in led by a grinning court official. She saw the five friends and tugged herself free, trotting the few metres across to them.

They swarmed round her, hugging her in every direction as they half-laughed, half-cried their welcome. Jeff stood and watched while behind them the crowd cheered and clapped, and the usher's cries for silence went ignored.